Elvis in Aspic

Gordon DeMarco

WCC

West Coast Crime

Portland, Oregon

First West Coast Crime Edition 1994

Manufactured in the United States of America.

Publisher's Cataloging-in-Publication Data
DeMarco, Gordon, 1944-
     Elvis in Aspic / Gordon DeMarco
     I. Title
PS3554.E448E48   1994
813.54--dc20   93-61107

ISBN 1-883303-11-7

Special thanks to Ryan Manwiller and Teresa Kosztics for all their patience and assistance.

For my father. We didn't agree on much of anything when it came to politics, but his unqualified support and encouragement of my writing was a rock that anchored me through all the lean times I have known.

Chapter 1

The tiny community of Turlock, a small agricultural town in California's San Joaquin Valley, has long been known for one thing—turkeys. It is a leading processor and packager of turkeys. Now, it is becoming famous as the home of the "Elvis Miracle."

Two weeks ago, Lester Lazar drove his 1964 Chevrolet Impala to his job at a local turkey processing plant, as he had done five days a week for the past thirteen years. When he came out to the parking lot at the end of the day he saw a group of workers standing in front of his car. Lester's heart sank. He feared his prize possession had been vandalized.

What he saw astounded him and the others. Reflecting off the candy apple red hood was the glowing silhouette of a human face. All agreed without hesitation that the face was none other than that of Elvis Presley.

"I was scared," said Lester. "The face was definitely Elvis'." Lazar and his coworkers said there was something hypnotic about the silhouette.

"It wasn't just the light," said Bill Dinkins, a worker at the turkey plant. "There was kind of a halo around Elvis' head. It was like a religious thing."

Lazar was too frightened to move his car. It has remained in the same spot since that first day. The silhouette appears on the hood of the car every day between the hours of four and six p.m.

As word spread, people began coming to the parking lot of the turkey plant to view the "Elvis miracle." By the third day more than four hundred had come to see the face of the King of Rock and Roll. By the end of the first week, some three thousand people had seen the face on the hood of Lester Lazar's Chevy.

A spokesman for the turkey factory said, "Originally, it was a nuisance. All these people in our parking lot. We thought we had a security problem on our hands. Now, well, the publicity has been great. We have started a new ad campaign linking our turkeys with Elvis. Orders are already up six percent."

Meanwhile, the local Catholic diocese has remained silent on the question on everyone's lips in the Turlock area these past two weeks—Is this a miracle? Will Lester Lazar's Chevy become an American version of the shrine at Lourdes, France? Time may tell.

I didn't like the ending, but I was in a hurry. I stored the text in my computer terminal and printed out a hard copy for my editor. It was my first Elvis story.

When I graduated from journalism school I thought the world would be my oyster, but there have been more barnacles than oysters in my world since I became a working journalist. I don't know, I thought Western Pennsylvania State had a pretty good journalism school. It's just that no one else did.

The only job I could get after graduation was with the Mahonning County *Shopping News*, across the border in Ohio. I didn't like Youngstown and I didn't like covering mall openings, so I quit after six months. I moved to upstate New York where I landed a job on a small town newspaper. It was a weekly and I worked the police beat. Mostly home burglaries and purse snatchings, but it did have its moments. Like the time a policeman shot and killed a teenager after a high-speed car chase. The police said the kid had a gun, but they tried very hard to bury the whole thing in a deep

6

hole. Yours Truly dug it up and got to the truth which blew the lid off a corrupt police force. I won a state journalism award for my stories and got fired, but not in that order.

I thought I had really arrived. Woodward and Bernstein, that was me. I was convinced I was on my way to investigative reporting stardom. I made a beeline to Manhattan and camped in the outer office of the New York *Times* with my award and a file folder full of my clips. That didn't impress anybody. The office was full of people from small town newspapers with journalism awards and file folders full of press clips.

It took me a week of sitting around the office and staring at photographs of the Sulzberger family mounted on the wall, but I finally got the message. Next, I went to the *Village Voice*. A guy who writes some of the movie reviews pretended to interview me just to be polite. He encouraged me to keep plugging away, but not at the *Voice*. He was awfully nice about it.

I worked my way down the chain with similar results. The *Daily News* threatened to call the security guard when I insisted on showing my clips to someone in authority. The *Post* wouldn't even let me sit down in the reception area. And the Long Island *Weekly* told me they didn't expect anything to open up for at least a year.

I guess this is all an explanation or maybe an apology for how I ended up at the *National COMET*. A lot of things happened between New York and the *COMET*. Mostly, it was just the passage of time, with the exception of a temporary replacement stint at the Los Angeles *Times*. I've been at the *COMET* for more years than I care to remember. Anything more than a couple of months is more than most of the staff at the *COMET* cares to remember. Ask around.

I've grown older, more depressed about some things and fairly cynical about all things. But it is a job. It may not be real journalism, but the *Post* or *Daily News* is?

A lot of people think we make up the stories that

are run in the *COMET*. With articles like the "Superglue Suicide," "Granny 72 Elopes with Boy 12," and "Killer Yogurt Leaves Two Dead," who can blame them? But, actually, a good many of the stories are true. Some were reported in the "legitimate" newspapers or taken off the wire. At the *COMET*, they are punched up and given goofy and lurid headlines. Some of the other stories are the products of fevered imaginations. It helps to have a fevered imagination if you work at the *COMET*.

Then there are the staple of diet articles, horoscopes, celebrity gossip columns and medical heart-pullers. Maybe it is all crap. Of course it is all crap, but it isn't a whole lot different from hundreds of so-called legitimate newspapers and magazines. They are sold in bookstores and newsstands. The *COMET* is found at the check-out counter at Safeway and Ralph's. Big deal.

I don't take crap from big city newspaper guys. Not anymore. Not since I became hip to the world of big time LA-San Francisco-New York journalism. A lot of bums work for the New York *Times*. Frisco has its share of gutter tabloid journalists who work for the *Chronicle*, which is just a jumped-up tabloid with a sports page. And LA is such a crazy place, it takes a certain number of twinkies and deranged at the *Times* to keep it honest. So, to hell with them and to hell with us. But, hey, if you can keep your sense of humor when all those about you are losing theirs, it's not so bad. When you really get to the bottom line, the difference between those of us who work on the tabloids and the "real," serious, big city journalists is that we *know* what we produce is entertainment. We don't have any pretensions. Some of us don't have much in the way of ethics, either, but as my editor would say, that is another can of soup.

Stan Barfyskowicz, the editor at the *COMET* had reassigned me to the "Elvis Beat." Sherman Bolivia is the self-appointed unofficial bureau chief of the Elvis watch. Sue Braska claims he invented the "Elvis is Alive" movement. Not that he believes Elvis is alive, it was just another of his many contributions to the world of journalism. If the tabloids could take on a human form, Sherman Bolivia could be the poster boy. He's fat, bald, and on the long side of fifty, a bad-dresser, a loud-talker, and a man who doesn't let things ethical inter-fere with his lifestyle. And he has these hands that look like Virginia hams when they make a fist, which they often do. Sherm is the kind of guy who likes to pound the air, desks and peoples' shoulders.

Sue "City" Braska is Sherm's opposite, as well as his opposition on most things. She is somewhere in her forties and worked for a big Midwestern daily about ten years ago. Something happened there which she has never talked about and she ended up at the *COMET*. Sue is a professional. She approaches a story for the *COMET* the same way she did for her former newspa-per. Like the stories she did about an eight-year-old girl who gave birth to Siamese quads or the one about the man with no arms who married the woman with no legs. To her a story was a story and it was her job to report it.

Sue would never make up a story out of nothing. Sherman almost always does. Sometimes they fight about it, but the *COMET* is not exactly the best place to debate ethics in journalism.

"Toast!" I heard my name being called. "Called" may be too polite a word. It came crashing through the walls of the editor's office. Stan Barfyskowicz—every-one calls him "Barfman," but not to his face—is the twentieth century's alternative to the telephone. "Why phone someone when you got a good pair of lungs?" the Barfman must have said a hundred times. "It gets their attention and puts the fear of God in 'em at the same time." It got my attention, but the only fear I had was the fear of going deaf. My desk was just outside the Barfman's door.

"Toast!" he hollered again. "Get your white ass in here." He always says that, too. It is always, "get your white ass in here," even though white asses are the only kind there are on the *COMET* staff. Sometimes when yelling for Sherm Bolivia he says, "Get your greasy white ass in here." Only Sue City Braska ever dared talk back. If she was busy she'd holler right back at him. If he insisted she would shout that if he wanted to see her he should "put his kielbasa back into his pants and sit on it" until she was free. After a couple of kielbasa comments the Barfman stopped hollering for her. Now, if he wants to see her, he finds some excuse to come out into the city room and casually approaches her like he is on his way to somewhere else. He called her on the office phone line once. At least that was the rumor that circulated at the time.

"What'd you do this time, Toast?" said Sherm Bolivia, already lining up against me in a boss-employee confrontation that hadn't even started. Yet.

"I'll let you know the minute I find out, Sherman."

"Probably for dicking off again. You college boys kill me. You finish that story I fed you last week?"

"What story?"

"That lady psychic I set you up with."

"Ah, yes. Zythia Zanatrope. Claims citizens from Saturn have colonized California and have captured key positions in state government. She believes they run the Department of Motor Vehicles."

"That's a great feed I gave you, Toast. Don't tell me you blew it."

"Zythia took an acid trip in 1968 and never came back. She should be in a home."

"So?"

"So, she was considerably less credible than the average ward case whose stories we run every week."

"Hey, college boy, ya gotta go with what ya got."

"Words that should be forever chipped in card-board."

"Ah, screw you. How's your Elvis story coming? Blow that one, too?"

I waved the copy in my hand. "I'm on my way in to see the Barfguy right now."

Sherm cocked his finger at me. "Don't go getting big-headed, Toast. Elvis is my department. I just gave

10

you some of my overload."

"Did I forget to say thank you?"

"Always willing to do a favor for a junior colleague. Just as long as he's grateful."

"I'm grateful, Sherm. I'm grateful."

Sherm Bolivia smiled and slapped me on the back. "Good. Glad to help out a junior colleague. Anytime."

"Now that we've settled that, can I get on with the rest of my life?"

"Sure, Toast. I just like a grateful guy, that's all."

"Toast! I want Toast!" The Barfman's third and, you could bet, final call.

I gave Sherman a little salute and turned away. I walked into the editor's office.

Stan Barfyskowicz was hunched over his desk like a leopard waiting for a gazelle to pass his way. "I told you guys to knock before you come in here," he barked.

I looked back at the open door. "It was wide open."

"I don't care,"

"You want me to go outside and close it so we can start all over again?"

"Forget it. I just want you to tell me something, Toast."

"Anything."

"See this sign?" He picked up the polished metal sign at the front of his desk. "Can you read what it says?

"I only went to a second-rate college in Pennsylvania. I might have trouble with some of the words."

"It says: Stanley Barfyskowicz, editor. You know what 'editor' means?"

"It means you make more money than the rest of us."

"It means the guy who's in charge of everybody else. The guy who makes the assignments and sets the deadlines. Stuff like that."

"Right. Thank you for sharing your job description with me, Stan." I began to back away and actually turned to leave.

11

"Toast!" That voice nailed my shoes to the ugly linoleum floor. "I'm not through with you. I want to know what's happened to your stories. Deadline was an hour ago. I'm holding up this week's edition for you. Where are they?"

I walked to the Barfman's desk. I gripped the end nearest me with my hands and stared directly into his sweaty, reddened face.

"That psychic was a donut hole. Nothing there. As for the Elvis story, I'm having trouble with it, especially the ending."

"Trouble? I don't recognize the word 'trouble'. The only word I recognize around here is 'Can do'."

"Isn't that two words?"

"I don't know what your problem is, Toast." The Barfman jerked his thumb to an embroidered sampler mounted on the wall behind his head. "See that?" It read— "The only difference between news and novels is plot."

"I didn't ask you write a goddamn novel, Toast," he said. "Just one of your usual first-rate stories. People are still talking about that piece you did on the man with the fungus on his face. That guy with the toad-stool kisser."

I looked at the floor. I don't mind writing trash. In fact, at times, I even like it. But I didn't have to stand in my editor's office and be praised for it.

"Ah, forget it, Toast. Just give me what you got. No one is going to care one way or the other about the ending. If it's a real smeller, we'll just cut it off. Besides, I've got more important fish to filet with you."

"What?" I was surprised the Barfman's tongue-lashing was so brief. There were at least two more plaques on the wall containing the best of journalism's pop philosophy. You hadn't been properly dressed down by the Barfman until he gave you a lecture tour of his office walls. For him to drop things just like that was a bit of a shock. "Are you on drugs, Stan?" I asked with some degree of seriousness.

"Here's the pitch, Toast. The Elvis thing is growing

12

like the Blob. At first I thought it was just a fad, but there are thousands of crazies out there—millions—who can't get enough of King Corn Pone. To get right down to the brass balls, we're getting beat to death by the competition. I mean like everybody. The *Sun, Inquirer, The World News.* Everybody is kicking our butt on Elvis stories. I mean we totally missed out on Lisa Marie's baby. The competition took that one right to the bank."

I shrugged my shoulders. "Why tell me? Sherm has the Elvis beat."

Barfyskowicz got up from his chair and walked to the door. He returned to his desk and took out a portable radio from one of the drawers. He turned it on and fooled with the dial until he found an all-news station. He set the radio in the middle of the desk and turned up the volume. There was a live broadcast of a big raid taking place on a crack house in East LA.

The Barfman put his hand on my shoulder and spoke in a low, growly voice. "That's the point, Toast. I love Sherm like a brother. There's nothing I wouldn't do for the man."

"Then why are you acting like the room is bugged. I feel like I'm in the middle of a bad spy movie."

Barfyskowicz put his finger to his lips. "Can't be too careful in the newspaper business. Leaks can kill."

The all-news station followed up with a story about the resignation of a cabinet secretary and a segment on dirt gardening.

"Leaks, schmeaks. What's this all about, Stan? I've got work to do."

The Barfman fluttered his hands in an attempt to calm me down. "I know you do, Toast. And that's the bottom page. I'd be the last to criticize the work of Sherman Bolivia. The absolute last."

"But," I said, trying to help him over the bridge.

"But our Elvis desk has gotten stale. Know what I mean?"

"Other than the story I just did, I don't pay much attention to Elvis. Is he still dead?"

"Funny, Toast. Look, I'll cut to the hunt. I need some new blood on the Elvis desk. Someone with some...." He stopped and made a punching gesture with his fist.

"Someone to undercut ol' Sherm."

"Hell no! Are you crazy? This is a two-man desk. Has been for a long time, I just didn't see it. I'm upgrading it. But I don't want just any slob to come aboard. I want you, Toast. I think you are the one man around here who can pump some new blood into this key area of the paper. Bring up the circulation, stuff like that."

I would have been flattered, but he called me a slob, didn't he? The Barfman thrust his hand at me. I jumped back. He smiled. "I knew I could count on you, Steve. You're beautiful people." He grabbed my hand and shook it.

"Have you talked to Sherm about this?"

Barfyskowicz turned away and looked at the radio. A traffic report came through the sound of whirling chopper blades. "I, uh, wanted to check it out with you first. I'll post a memo later."

"You're right. The direct approach is the best policy."

"Yeah. Look, Toast, there's something else."

"If you want me to try another one of our advertisers idiotic weight-loss scams, I quit right now. That stewed tomatoes-and-liver diet nearly killed me."

The Barfman leaned back in his chair and began to laugh. He built it up to a roar in no time. "No, nothing like that." He wiped the tears from the corner of his eyes with his palms. "Stewed tomatoes and liver for thirty mother-grabbing days. How the hell did you ever do it, Toast?"

"You said you'd fire me if I didn't. Remember?"

Barfyskowicz had a whimsical and far away look in his eye like he was thinking of the dog he had when he was a boy or the last time he got laid. "Yeah, what a great laugh that was."

"Stan. You said there was something else."

14

"Ah," he said, coming out of it. He reached into his pocket and pulled out a folded piece of paper. He buried it in his fist. "I've got a lead on an Elvis story that is so hot that it could burn a hole in a concrete floor.

"He hasn't been seen bowling again over at Colony Lanes, has he?"

A near-angry sneer reshaped the Barfman's lips. "Shit, no. This is serious stuff. Real serious stuff. Like the Kennedy assassination, only maybe bigger."

I looked hard into his eyes. A story about a boy with cerebral palsy who was training for a five-kilometer run topped the local news roundup on the all-news station. "You are still on drugs, aren't you?"

"Cut that shit out," he said, angrily as he passed me the folded piece of paper.

"What's this?"

"Deep Throat. A potential ticket to a four-million circulation. Fame and recognition for all of us. Or who knows, maybe squat."

I unfolded the small piece of paper. There was nothing on it other than a seven-digit number. A phone number, I thought. The phone number of yet another poor, deranged sod who had proof that aliens from outer space were controlling our brain waves or that he was himself an alien who wanted to come in from the cold and spill the beans on an intergalactic conspiracy to take over the planet. I had heard it all before.

"Don't judge, Toast," the Barfman said, springing to the defense of the seven-digit number. "I get ten thousand phone calls a year. Ninety-nine percent of them are from certified whackos. I've gotten to know just what kind of whacko they are after two sentences. About one-in-ten is good for a story. The other nine are coming from or going to the bughouse. I can tell all that in the time it takes to give a midget a blow job."

I rolled my eyes. The all-news station was into its afternoon magazine format. A psychic travel agent was being interviewed. I wished I was there, wherever it was he was talking about.

"But I think this guy is on the level," the Barfman

15

continued. "He called me for a solid week before I would talk to him. The guy is some kind of researcher. I forget. But he knows his onions. I did some checking on what he told me."

"You checked on a source?"

"Laugh if you want, but if what this guy has got turns out to be the McGill, it... it could change all our lives." His eyes grew big and gazed at the wall. He looked like he was about to meet the Wizard of Oz.

"Stan, I'm going to speak to your doctor and have him cut back on your medication."

"He believes the CIA killed Elvis!"

I reached for the phone on the Barfman's desk. "What is your doctor's number? You could be having a serious episode."

Chapter 2

I could tell by the look in the Barfman's eyes that this story had the potential to be his story of stories. The one editors dream about. It didn't matter to him whether it would turn out to be true or not. It was a story that could grow legs. Big, strong legs. And it was to be my job to develop it so it could run the distance. Run and win! Win for the *COMET*. Sell more papers than had ever been sold before. Make more money than had ever been made before. I could see it all in his eyes—the headlines and dollar signs. It was no use to try and discuss it with him or try to talk him back down to planet earth. The CIA had killed Elvis and that was the lead. Now go find the facts. "That's the way we do things around here," he would say when anyone would question one of his harebrained ideas. "That's what we do. That's who we are."

I went downstairs to the *COMET* library. The *COMET* has a first-rate clipping and photo library that would embarrass a lot of big city newspapers. Not that it is state of the art technology. It isn't. Nothing is computerized or data-based. It is just big. Bound volumes of the *COMET* going back to the creation. The *COMET*'s creation. And clipping files from the mainstream press on every cockamamie story that ever had the nerve to jump into print.

The library was the result of a decade's labor by

the chief librarian. As a librarian, Shelly Bubblefarb is something of a cross between Gracie Allen and the head guy at the Library of Congress. She knows her business better than anyone in the business. The problem comes in trying to figure out her system.

If you were looking for the file on Siamese twins, you would find it under "Thailand", or maybe "Southeast Asia". If you wanted to look through the file on Bigfoot sightings you could probably find it filed under "Health care, foot." Once I tried to find what we had on microwaves that turn food into gold. It is a story that pops up in the tabloids from time to time. I looked under "Microwaves," "Gold," and "Food," but couldn't find it. Shelly, who doesn't really like for people to go through her files unassisted, stood by with her hands on her wide hips while I searched in vain. After twenty minutes I asked for her help.

"Look under 'Sheldon'," she said, dismissively, like it was the most obvious place to look.

"Sheldon?" I said. "Why Sheldon?"

"My brother Sheldon. He bought me my first microwave."

The Elvis files were easier to locate. The trouble was there were so many of them. They had their own Bubblefarb sub-heading cross-referencing system. There were files organized by geographic region, concerts he gave, women he was involved with, his family ("Look under 'Vernon', his father"), sightings after death, further subdivided under malls, supermarkets and musical events. There were headings for the cars he owned, the names of his closest associates, songs recorded both before and after death and personal spiritual experiences people had with the King of Rock and Roll. There were others, but I was just on a random schmooz to learn a little something about the King, who had a significant life experience on August 16, 1977. Most people say he died on that date. Others say he faked his death and went into hiding. I didn't know one way or the other. I lost interest in Elvis sometime after "Blue Suede Shoes" and before the Beatles. I needed some background.

Shelly came over to where I was rummaging through the files and planted her feet. She looked at me like I had just been caught stealing money from her change purse. "Finding everything today, boychick?" she said. She was a Jewish mother without the charm. She treated everyone who came into her library—dubbed "Bubblerama" by Sherm Bolivia—like a child. But she wasn't old enough to be a real Jewish mother. She is approaching thirty-five. The nasties in the celebrity gossip department liked to say, "But no one is sure from which direction she is approaching it." She is large and uses a lot of make-up. Her hair is black and curly. Her voice is loud. Even when she whispers it's loud. And it has a rasp to it that makes her sound like a socket wrench. She overdresses, too, if the truth be told. But underneath all that beats a heart of a nice person. That's what I tell myself every time I step across the threshold and into Bubblerama. "Just grazing through the Elvis files," I said in answer to her question.

"I run a library here, Toast, not a cattle ranch. What are you looking for? Shelly will get it for you." She was the type who almost always referred to herself in the third person.

"Just general stuff, really. I want to catch up on Elvis, especially since he died."

"Well, what? Sightings by middle age housewives in Michigan? Out of body experiences by anorexic teenagers? How about his latest recordings? Shelly's got it all right here." She patted one of the file drawers. As she talked her fingers and arms flew over the drawers, opening them and snatching a file or two and closing them. She repeated this motion several times as smoothly and effortlessly as Ted Williams used to play caroms off the left field wall at Fenway. Without looking at me, she laid the folders into my hands as she moved up and down the rows of file drawers. It was all I could do to keep up with her.

"Here's one that might interest you," she said,

handing me the manila folder. "New medical evidence that Elvis is alive."

She handed me the folder. I glanced at the file heading "Ohio." I knitted my eyebrows. "Why Ohio?" I foolishly asked.

"A doctor in Cincinnati. It was the first story on the subject that I clipped." She took the folder from me and opened it. "Here, look, Toast."

The article was from the Cincinnati daily. It was a small two-column job. The headline ran—"Local Doctor Claims Elvis Death Cause A Cover-up."

Shelly pulled a few more files for me to look at. "There," she said, dusting her hands. "You can graze on these for awhile. Remember, any questions, Shelly's here to help. And you can pass that on to those slobs in Gossip."

"Say what?"

"Shanks and his girls. They sneak around here deliberately trying to misfile things. I'll bust the humps of the next one I catch doing that." She made a fist and pounded it into the palm of her other hand like she meant it. She wouldn't leave me alone until I promised to convey her message. It wasn't the first time she had issued such threats to members of the staff. Sherm called them "Bubblegrams" . They were mostly bluff, but we all knew that one day she would catch someone in the act—*in flagrante bubblictis*, as Sherm called it— and make them pay the price. A lot of people at the *COMET* hoped Sherm would be the first one.

I spent the next two hours at the reading table looking through Elvis Presley's life-after-death. Actually, the clippings revealed a lot more about the desperate people who claimed to have seen Elvis, talked to him or starred him in their dreams in which he said or did something that had profoundly affected their waking lives. Americans have a hard time letting go of heroes. I mean kings don't die easily, especially the big ones like the King of Kings and the King of Rock and Roll.

Shelly brought me a cup of coffee. It was another of

the services you got in the library. It's fine if you're a coffee drinker, but that doesn't matter to Shelly. You get coffee whether you want it or not. And she stands there until you take a sip and pay her a compliment. The compliment part is easy, but if you don't like coffee, it is that first sip that's the hard part.

"Ah, wonderful," I lied, swallowing that first deadly gulp. "Mountain- grown Jamaican, isn't it?"

Shelly smiled. "No, today's house blend is a dark French roast."

I took another small sip. "Yes, of course."

"There's plenty more where that came from, Toast." She motioned to the coffee maker in her office.

I held up my hand. "Only one cup for me, Shelly. Doctor's orders."

"Doctor, schmocter. What does he know? Coffee is good for you. Does your Mister Doctor know that coffee was originally used as an elixir to cure body ailments?

"I don't know. I will ask the next time I go in for my caffeine extraction treatments."

"Your what?"

"Nothing." I looked at my watch. "God, is it that late already?" I jumped to my feet. "Got some stories to file, Shelly. Thanks for all your help." I stacked the Elvis folders on the table and turned to leave.

"Toast!" Shelly Bubblefarb barked at my back. I stopped in my tracks and turned around. She was pointing at my nearly full cup of coffee on the table. "Your coffee."

"Right." I picked it up and walked out of Bubblerama. I dumped the coffee in the first water fountain I came to without breaking stride.

Chapter 3

I returned to the news room. Sherm tried to tell me a joke as I passed his desk. He had been trying to tell me the same joke for a week. I always cut off Sherm Bolivia when he tries to tell jokes. It is sort of a principle with me. Without exception, his jokes are dirty, lame, ethnically repulsive and occasionally racist. Sherm is one of those people who has the uncanny knack to pick out jokes that represent the basest aspect of the culture and goes around sharing it with everyone he can make eye contact with. A good many people who have worked at the *COMET* for more than a few months have learned never to allow Sherm Bolivia to make eye contact with them.

However, Sherm has his fellow connoisseurs of bad taste on the staff. It is my good fortune that none of them work within hearing range of my desk.

I sat at my VDT listlessly filing a story about the inventor of plastic vomit. One of the Valley papers had dug him up when he was on a visit out here and did a story on him. I tracked him down and did a ten-minute phone interview with him.

The man sounded eccentric enough to have actually invented plastic vomit. And plastic dog shit, too, as he reminded me three times during the course of the interview. He was a man who was very proud of his accomplishments and he let me know it. Some people invent electric lights and the heart-lung machine. Others invent plastic vomit and dog poo. It's that kind of world.

I timed my work on the story to run past quitting time. Both Sherm and Sue City left around five. Stan Barfyskowicz had disappeared earlier in the afternoon. The news room wasn't quite empty, but it did provide the privacy I wanted to make my phone call.

I reached into my pocket for the phone number the Barfman had given me. I unfolded it and tucked its top edge under my phone. I looked at it while I punched the finishing touches on the plastic vomit man.

I turned off the terminal and stared at the phone number. I didn't want to dial it and I really didn't look forward to talking to another loon. But who was I to make such a judgment? Hadn't I just interviewed the man who invented styrene puke?

I counted off four "ringy-dingies." I was going to give it two more and then bail out. On the sixth ring the receiver was picked up.

"Hello?" I said. There was no answer on the other end. "Hello," I repeated.

"Who's this?" demanded a suspicious male voice. "How did you get this number?"

"My name is Steve Toast. I work for the *National COMET*. My editor gave me your number. Stan Barfyskowicz. He said he talked with you."

"How can I be sure you are who you say you are?"

It was a question I had encountered dozens of times in the business. Their response to my response usually tipped me off as to the competency of the other party.

"I have identification," I said. "I am taking out my wallet. Here is my California driver's license. The number is N 10987356. The physical description matches mine and there is a picture of me—Steven S. Toast."

There was a slight pause at the other end. "What are you, some kind of comedian? Look at me, Toast, I'm not laughing. I want to know who you are. I've got to be careful who I talk to. I'm a marked man."

"Who marked you, Mr., uh? What's your name, friend?"

"Now wouldn't you like to know?"

He had at least passed the first test. You'd be surprised how many people have been satisfied to have me read my driver's license over the telephone. But that only meant that he wasn't a certifiable head case. I still figured I had a live one on the line.

"Mr. Barfyskowicz says you have some information that suggests the Central Intelligence Agency might possibly have been responsible—"

"Stop right there! You fool! Don't you realize my phone is tapped? I am in great danger for what I know, but I'll be damned if I'm going to make it any easier for the bastards. Are you there, Javert? Are you listening? You bastard!"

"Javert? I told you my name is Toast."

"But the Company bloodhound stalking me is named Javert."

"How do you know that?"

"It's my business to know."

"Can we meet and talk about all this? At some neutral, non-bugged place of your preference, of course."

"I will call you from a phone booth in ten minutes. Where are you?"

"I'm at the *COMET*. My number is—" The phone clicked dead.

I sat at my chair going through my article assignments for the coming weeks. Same old stuff. The wife who put gunpowder in her abusive husband's birthday cake and sent him into the ozone; the vampire prairie dogs of West Texas; and the trees that terrorized a town. The Barfman had attached a handwritten note to the tree story. "Set it in Idaho. Boise area. Was there once. Nice town." There were other stories, but I didn't get past the terrorist trees.

The phone rang. It was the Elvis man. He told me to meet him at Lanny's Donuts in Inglewood. I told him it would take me forty-five minutes to get there. More if

24

the traffic was snarled. He told me to step on it. Actually, what he said was, "Put your pedal to the metal." God, I hoped he wasn't the kind who drives a pickup truck with a CB radio, wears a baseball cap and calls people "good buddy." Somehow, I didn't think he would be.

Chapter 4

It took me an hour to drive the twenty-three miles to Lanny's Donuts. And that was twenty-three freeway miles. I took the Hollywood south to the Ventura; the Ventura west to the San Diego; and the San Diego south to the Marina Freeway. I got off at Slauson and from there it was less two miles to Lanny's. Lanny's is the kind of place you can see long before you get there. It has a thirty-foot *papier-mache* donut on its roof.

On the other hand, a thirty-foot donut wasn't going to help me recognize my Elvis contact. I hadn't asked what he looked like and he didn't know me, so I didn't know what I was looking for. I got out of the car carrying a copy of the *COMET*. I held it out in front of me with both hands.

There is a scene in *The Third Man* where Baron von Kurtz telephones Holly Martins, Harry Lime's pal who has come to Vienna to see him. Martins is a writer of pulp westerns. The Baron, a friend of the just "deceased" Lime asks Martins to meet him at the Cafe Mozart. When Martins asks him how they will know each other, the Baron tells him he will be carrying one of Martins' books. The scene of the well-dressed Baron walking through the the patio of Vienna's most fashionable cafe conspiculously holding out a copy of *The Oklahoma Kid* has stuck with me all these years. Ever since I first saw the film, I have wanted to meet some-

26

one that way. Now I had my chance.

I strolled slowly through Lanny's parking lot displaying the *COMET* like a circus poster. The 96-point headline read—"Teenage Girl Gives Birth To Sheep." A man walked up to me. I started to say something. He reached into his pocket. My heart missed a beat. My mind wanted to turn and run, but my feet had no idea what was going on.

"Are you the man I talked to on the phone?" I stammered.

The man squinted one eye as he continued to dig into his pocket.

"Elvis Presley?" I whispered.

The man pulled his hand out of his pocket. He opened his fist and revealed two quarters and several pieces of smaller change. "Lemme get a paper from you, buddy," he said, counting the coins in his hand.

My heart started beating again. "This isn't a newspaper," I said. "This is the *COMET*." I pushed him aside and walked into the dinner.

A man in the corner stood halfway up in a booth and nodded his head for me to join him. Unless he was another *COMET* reader, I figured I had found my man.

I walked slowly to his booth, still not totally convinced he was the man I was to meet. He was wearing what used to be a suit a long time ago. It was shiny and black and had more wrinkles than a California prune. He was wearing a white shirt that still had some life in it and a tie that was dark and narrow and had gone out of style thirty years ago. His hair was combed, but probably not recently and he wore at least a day's growth of beard on his face. If Ralph Nader had a brother, I felt I was just about to meet him.

"Sit down, Toast," he said. I sat down. The man took a large, nervous gulp of coffee from the cup sitting in front of him. A half-eaten jelly donut sat on a paper plate next to the coffee. He followed his swallow with a savage bite out of the donut. Through a full mouth he began speaking.

"Now, let's see that driver's license, wiseguy." I

smiled and produced my wallet from my hip pocket. I pulled out my driver's license and flicked it toward him. He picked it up and began examining it like a Turkish customs agent. A full minute later he tossed it back at me. I wiped off the jelly and returned it to the plastic sleeve in my wallet.

"Satisfied?" I asked. "Or do you want to see my K Mart charge card?"

"Save it, Toast. This isn't the Johnny Carson Show."

"Look, pal, you're talking to the *National COMET*, not the Washington *Post*. My name's Toast, not Woodward or Bernstein."

"Screw Woodward and Bernstein. And screw the *Post*, too. All of them are stuck together with CIA peanut butter. If I wanted to talk to the CIA, the Watergate boys would be the first ones I'd go to. But me and the Company aren't exactly friends. They're trying to kill me."

"Do I have time for a coffee?"

The left side of his face sneered. He started to get up. "And I don't have time for comedians. Your editor said you wanted the story. Screw him and screw you and that rag you work for." He nearly spit a gob on the *COMET* that I had laid on the table. He was halfway out of the booth before I stopped him.

"Hold on, fella. I didn't mean anything. Come on, sit down." I reached across the table and gently pushed his shoulder down. He sat. "Look, since we're both here, how about we talk?" I slid to the end of the booth. "You could use a fresh cup and a new donut. Let me get it." I stood up.

"Bring me a Bismarck," he said.

"You got it." I walked to the counter and got two coffees, a Bismarck and a cruller. I didn't want the coffee, but Lanny's isn't the kind of place you can order tea and get away with it.

I returned to the booth and sat one of the coffees in front of the man in the has-been suit. I watched him empty a canister of sugar into it. He would have made

28

a great policeman.

I bit into my cruller. "Okay," I said. "The CIA is after you. There's a lot of that going around. But assuming you are right, you want to get your story into print before they come down on you, right?"

"You got a smart mouth, Toast. Just because your fishwrapper subsists on fantasies from dingalings, doesn't mean I'm one. Get that through your head."

I nodded. "Maybe. But why come to a dingaling rag like the *COMET*?"

The man looked at me impatiently. "What? Am I talking to myself? I told you the *Post* is CIA. The *Times*, both here and New York and just about every big time newspaper you can think of is connected. Some are controlled from the top down, You don't believe me? Check it out. September 1977. *Rolling Stone* broke the story that American journalists had been linked to the CIA for more than twenty-five years. More than seven hundred of the bastards secretly shared information and/or provided operational assistance to the CIA. And you think I'm paranoid. It's the rest of you that are blind to what's been going on in this country."

I remembered the story about the CIA journalists. I was in college at the time. We discussed it in my "Ethics in Journalism" class. Everybody thought it stunk—the CIA journalists, not the class—and a lot of us were spooked about getting jobs where we might be working next to or for people who were intelligence agents. But it was only a six-week course and when it ended, so did a lot of the the ethical outrage and career panic.

So, the Elvis man wasn't a raving looney, but the look in his eye and the feverish pitch to his voice told me he wasn't exactly a bank loan officer, either. He began sweating as he started to spin his story.

"What do you think Iran-Contra was all about? Some gung ho Marine colonel doing a solo? For God's sake, man, the Christic Institute was right. Only they didn't go far enough. The Secret Team has been running the foreign policy of this country ever since the

Bay of Pigs. CIA cowboys, anti-Castro Cubans and a handful of military brass hats who traffic in arms and drugs. I'm not making this up. Damn it, it was on nationwide TV . The Congressional hearings. Secord, Singlaub, Shackley, Clines. And there were others. Remember Edwin Wilson? He sold arms and explosives to Khaddafi. Wilson's only problem was he got caught. The Bay of Pigs, the JFK hit, Watergate, Iran-Contra. Hell, those are the only ones where they screwed up. Got caught with their hand in the cookie jar. Do you know how many other operations there were? Operations that succeeded and no one knows about?"

I held up my hand. "Time out!" If I had had a whistle I would have blown it. The Elvis man stopped in his tracks. He hunched over the table and picked up his coffee cup with both hands. They shook as he took a gulp that could have been heard in the parking lot.

"This is all very interesting," I said. "But if we are going to talk about the history of CIA dirty tricks, we will have to send out for sleeping bags and cigarettes. My editor said you think the CIA croaked Elvis Presley. That's what I want to know about."

"It doesn't do any good unless you understand the big picture. Tie it all together. Otherwise, it sounds like a hallucination. I am not hallucinating. I want you to know that. I've never taken drugs in my life. If I could find a doctor I could trust, you could have me tested. I'm straight and sober. I've tumbled to another one of the Secret Team's operations and they are going to kill me for what I know."

"What makes you think—"

"What makes me think they will kill me? Is that what you want to know? I'll tell you what. Do you know how many witnesses involved in the JFK assassination died within three years?" He didn't give me a chance to shake my head one way or another. "53%, that's how many. A statistical and actuarial impossibility. I could go on, but I think you get my drift. If the Company thinks you know too much and can cause them grief, they will arrange for you to die. It will be a fall on the stairs or an auto accident on the freeway or a manufactured heart attack. They're clever bastards and they don't fool around. When your number is pulled, you can believe me, they will pay you a visit. A visit from which you will have to be carried away in a black plastic bag."

"You sound pretty sure of this."

"The Company will get me. Tomorrow, next week, next month. Next year, if I am extremely lucky. But sooner or later they will get me. It's what they do best. I want to get the story to someone before I'm history. Someone I can trust. You can tell how desperate I must be to be talking to a tabloid reporter. And one named Toast at that."

"Hey! Speaking of names, what's yours?"

He brushed his hand across his chest. "That doesn't matter."

"It does to me. I like to know who I'm talking to. Funny, but that's the kind of guy I'm."

"Coates," the man whispered.

"Coates?"

"Yeah, Coates. Something wrong with that?

"Not at all. I'm sitting in a joint with a thirty-foot donut on the roof talking to a guy named Coates who thinks the CIA is going to murder him because he knows it killed Elvis Presley. No, your name is about the only normal thing I've heard in the last twenty minutes."

"Yeah, yeah, life is strange. You want to hear this story or what?"

"Let me get out my notebook." I reached inside my jacket for pen and note pad. I looked at Coates when I was ready. His eyes had grown smaller. Fiercer. He looked puzzled.

"Where's the dough?" he asked.

"The what?"

"Your editor said there would be a payment for my story."

I put the note pad back into my pocket. "He didn't say anything to me about it."

"The lousy bastard!"

"Yeah, a lot of us at the *COMET* feel the same way

about him."

"What are we going to do? I need the dough to split. My place is getting too hot. The Company got me fired from my job months ago. It takes cash to stay a step ahead of them."

"I'm sorry, Coates. I really don't know anything about a payment."

"Call your editor."

I shook my head. "When the Barfman leaves the office, he leaves the known world. I won't be able to contact him until tomorrow."

"Damn! I need some get-away money. I was planning on going into to hiding as soon as I straighten a few things out."

"My hands are tied, old man. There's nothing I can do."

Coates turned quickly in his seat and looked looked over his shoulder. "Is this a setup? You're with the Company. This is the visit, isn't it?"

I held up my hands and tried to calm him. He was ten seconds away from hysteria. "Hold on, friend. No set up. No CIA visit. Honest. Just another one of the *COMET*'s many screwups. Come on, sit down." He slowly eased himself back into the booth. "Can I freshen up your coffee?" He shook his head no.

"Look, Toast, I have nowhere to go. My time is running out. I don't want this story to die with me. But I can't just give it to your rag. You know what I mean?"

"I can try to get some money from my editor, but you should know, regardless of what he told you, he isn't going to pay for something unless he knows what he is buying. Give me something to take back to him. Give me something to tease him with."

Coates scratched his chin and stared past me. He began picking apart his empty styrofoam coffee cup, piece by tiny piece. "A teaser," he uttered, like he was hearing the word for the very first time.

He cleared his throat. "The CIA murdered Elvis," he said, "because he knew the details of the Company plot to assassinate Carter."

Journalists are trained to maintain poker faces when interviewing sources and covering live stories. Even those of us in the gutter tabloids are supposed to wear blank faces when contacts tell us their outrageous tales. But this one caught me off-guard. I raised my eyebrows. Actually, they jumped like they were looking for a place to hide in my hair.

"Jimmy Carter?" I asked, more incredulous than skeptical.

Coates nodded. "That's the one. Mr. Peanut. The President of the United States."

I whistled through my teeth. "Now, that's what I call a teaser. How did Elvis know about any CIA plot to kill the President?"

"James Earl Ray told him."

"The guy who killed Martin Luther King?" I said reflexively. My eyebrows ran screaming out of Lanny's and hid under a car in the parking lot.

Coates nodded and smiled slightly. I had been teased and he knew it.

Chapter 5

I must have spent forty minutes on the San Pedro Freeway. It was stop-and-go all the way. Even at ten miles an hour I missed my exit. I had other things on my mind. I was fantasizing about Seymour Hersh breaking the My Lai massacre story and Mark Lane researching *Rush To Judgement* and Carl and Bob lifting the veils of Watergate. I thought about Peabody awards, Pulitzers and National Press Club luncheons.

And then I thought about the previous times I have had these kind of pipedreams and the subsequently identified nut cases who had cruelly fuelled them. And I thought about the man who looked like Ralph Nader's brother. The man I had spent the last hour with. The man who was probably a classic paranoid with persecution delusions. And I thought about conspiracy buffs, the computer nerds of politics. That's why I missed my exit.

I made my way to my flat in Venice by way of Culver City and Santa Monica. If you live on the old canals in Venice it can be quite nice. That is, if the mosquitoes aren't carrying malaria. The beach is something else. Muscle Beach and Bimbomania. Stoners, steroids and Sony Walkmen. Skateboarders, roller bladers, men wearing tee shirts that have scatalogical expressions printed across the front and well-oiled bodies of air-head blonds wearing g-string leotards and hair that looks like pan-fried noodles. Venice Beach is where a culture ends up when it dies and goes to hell.

Me, I live in this poured concrete housing estate neighborhood that must have been designed by Stalinist architects. Or the British. Rectangular apartment buildings all painted sea-sick green. A lot of the residents call the development the "Venice Gulag." But the lawns are nice and the rent is reasonable.

I spent that night in front of the television watching the Dodgers lose to the Cubs. Again. I went out to Ralph's Supermarket in the fifth inning to buy a deli food dinner. I finished off the game with a roast beef and mayo on an onion roll, a pickle and a half-pound of potato salad.

I didn't think about Coates or Elvis or Pulitzers until the news came on at eleven. In the middle of the broadcast there was a story about the death of one of Jimmy Carter's former advisers. He was one of those among the inner circle of Georgians whose name rarely made the news. I barely recognized the name and would have looked right past the story to the weather report, but something reached out and snagged my attention. It was the adviser's cause of death. He died in a car accident on the freeway. A freak car accident, the newscaster said.

I reached for the telephone without thinking, but it rang before I could pick it up. "You see the news, Toast?" the voice asked. It was Coates.

"Yeah. I'm watching it now."

"That was no freeway accident, believe me. Got enough teasers now?

"I think so."

"I'm out of my apartment five minutes ago. My number is no longer any good. I will tell you a number you can reach me when I find a safe one. I'll call you at the *COMET* tomorrow."

The phone clicked dead. He had just hung up, hadn't he? I mean it was his way, wasn't it? There wasn't anyone standing over him with a gun or anything, was there? I rang back just to make sure. The line was busy. I tried again and every five minutes for the next half hour. Still busy. Well, at least he was there.

I switched on the late movie. It was *Three Days of the*

35

Condor. I jumped out of my chair and turned on Leno. I went to bed after the first guest and tried to sleep. It wasn't as easy as it had been the night before.

Chapter 6

I arrived at the *COMET* a few minutes early the next day. On my way to my desk I made a slight detour to the celebrity gossip corner of the news room.

Armitage Shanks has been doing celebrity gossip columns almost as long as there have been celebrity gossip columns to do. He had been Hedda Hopper's protege forty years ago. Some back-stabbers in the business said he picked out the hats she wore. The really nasty ones said he wore them, too.

Armitage does wear hats. Big, outrageous hats. But, as far as I know, they are his own. He dresses like Quentin Crisp. In fact, he looks something like the old British queen who was so popular on the lecture circuit a few years back. I think, however, Armitage wears less rouge.

Armitage Shanks doesn't "work" at the *COMET*. Not in the traditional sense of the word. Rather, he holds court. He fixed up the celebrity gossip corner of the city room to look like the front parlor of a French brothel. Wall partitions were covered with a red-flocked velvet paper of a particularly lurid floral design. Desks and filing cabinets have been replaced by coffee tables, a chintz covered settee and a powder-blue mohair wing-back chair. Armitage's powder-blue mohair wing-back chair. That's where he works. The throne of his court. An antique phone sits on a table next to the mohair.

The phone is Armitage's equivalent of a word processor. He talks with the celebrities and then tells his three-person staff what they said. It is his staff who write down Armitage's words and comb Shelly Bubblefarb's library for celebrity photos. They also take turns making tea and buying the cookies and petit fours. Armitage always has a cup of tea and a bite-size sweet in his hand.

Lance, one of Armitage's staffers, was brewing a pot of tea and arranging cookies on a bone china plate. Armitage's office dishware probably cost more than the *COMET* computer system and he isn't shy letting people know just how much each piece cost.

"Steve, darling!" Armitage said in his best Tallulah Bankhead voice. He extended a beringed hand in a way that begged for it to be kissed. I just waved instead.

"Armitage," I grinned. "How's tricks?"

A playful leer crossed his face. "You naughty boy. You know very well I gave up that sort of thing years ago. I am a respectable senior citizen these days."

"Shame on me." I paused and looked around for a moment before speaking again. "I come bearing a message. Do you promise not to shoot the messenger?"

Shanks pulled a face. "Would I shoot a colleague? Wait, I take that back. I do have a list, you know." He smiled and turned his head toward Lance, who was pouring boiling water into a teapot. "Lance, pour our dear friend a cup of tea." Lance wheeled a tea trolley next to Armitage's stuffed mohair and poured tea into two cups. He handed the first one to Armitage and the second one to me.

"I can't stay, Armitage. Really. I'm just delivering a message."

Shanks picked up the cup and brought it to his lips. He blew on the tea before taking a sip. "I hope your communique is not from the dread Miss Bubblefarb. I can't bear that woman."

I took a sip of tea before putting both cup and saucer very carefully on the tea trolley. "Uh, well, actually, it is."

Armitage rolled his eyes. "I should have guessed. I would dearly like to know what her problem is. She's too young to be going through menopause. Too young and too fat. She must have been abused as a child to possess a disposition like that."

"She just wants your staff to be a tad more careful when refiling material in the library."

Armitage swung his head toward Lance. "Did you hear that, Lance? Our Miss Bubblefarb wants us to be a tad more careful when refiling material in the library."

"Bitch!" Lance spit as he whisked away to a small desk on the other side of the flocked partition.

"Indeed." Armitage said, his voice trailing after Lance. "Please be sure to convey this most important Bubblegram to Scotty and Roy when they get here." Lance voiced his affirmation.

Armitage nibbled on a cookie and took a sip of tea. He looked at me. "You can tell Miss Piggy for us," he said coldly.

I held up my hand. "I really don't want to get into this, Armitage. Shelly asked me to pass her concern to you. I've done that. Now I'm out of it." I looked at my watch. "I've got to get to work." I turned and took a few steps before stopping. I turned back to Armitage. "Armitage, do you think Elvis Presley is alive?"

"What an odd question."

"No, really."

"Don't you read your own newspaper?"

"I'm serious."

"Dear boy, if Elvis Presley came back to the entertainment world a lot of people would be extremely upset about the fortunes they would lose on the 'Elvis Lives' merchandizing marathon. However, there would also be those who would kill each other to sign him up to recording contracts and concert tours."

"Is that a 'no'?"

"I will ask James Dean the next time he calls."

I smiled because I didn't know what else to do. I looked at my watch again and excused myself again. I backed out of his salon. I didn't bow, although I felt as if I should have.

I walked through the news room to my desk. Before I sat down I heard my name being yelled by Stan Barfyskowicz. I gathered up the mail from my pigeonhole on the way to answer the Barfman's summons.

I knocked on his door. He said "enter." I opened the door and walked in. Stupid ritual.

"You talk to Deep Throat, Toast?"

"Yeah. His name is Coates."

"Deep Coates!" Barfyskowicz roared with laughter at his own little joke. I smiled. It was a step up for him.

"Well? He have anything we can use?"

"Maybe. It's hard to tell."

"Maybe? You talked to him didn't you?"

"He wants money."

The Barfman leaned back in his chair. "Ah," he said, as if it had slipped his mind. "How much does the bastard want?"

"We didn't talk price. You didn't say anything to me about money."

"So, I forgot."

"Right. He thinks the CIA is out to murder him. He wants get away money. Get-out-of-town money."

"You mean get-out-of-town-with-my-money money."

"I don't know if what he has to sell is worth anything, but he seems truly frightened for his life. That much I am sure of."

"Well, we're not paying for being scared. What's he got? Are we talking major series or just another flake to put on the inside pages?"

"I don't know. He wouldn't tell me that much. But he does seem to know a lot about the CIA."

"Any fruitcake can read a book. Gimme something, Toast."

"He thinks the CIA killed Elvis because James Earl Ray told him about the Company's plot to assassinate Jimmy Carter."

The Barfman reached into the top drawer of his

desk and pulled out a half-empty pack of Kool cigarettes. He shook one out and put it between his lips. He
rifled through the drawer for matches. He found a book
and peeled off a match and lit his cigarette. He took an
enormous drag, tilted his head back and exhaled the
smoke toward the ceiling. He had a faraway look in his
eyes.

"How much is get-out-of-town money these days?"
he said. He reached for a pad of paper and took a pen
from his shirt pocket. He scribbled something on it and
ripped off the top sheet and passed it to me. "See how
far this will get him."

Chapter 7

When I got back to my desk the phone was ringing. It was Coates. When I told him the figure Barfyskowicz had written on the note pad, he nearly choked. He insisted that would only buy him a few days, a week at the most. He wanted more. Much more. I told him I would talk to the Barfman, but I couldn't promise anything. He wanted to call the whole thing off, but I convinced him to meet me again. He told me I would get only as much of the story as I paid for. Given the circumstances, it sounded fair to me. We agreed to meet later in the afternoon at a dive in Gardena.

I marched back into the Barfman's office to plead for more money, but he had left the building. There was no telling when he would return. I went to Accounting and drew out the money. I hoped it would buy me more than an hour in LA freeway traffic.

I spent the early afternoon working on one of my other story assignments. I was looking for an inspiration for the piece on the "terrorist trees." I was like a kid playing with his oatmeal. Actually, the story was rather routine. The "terrorism" was falling branches, roots pushing up through streets and sidewalks and paint-killing sap dripping on the hoods of expensive automobiles. Hardly The *Night of the Living Dead*, but that's the way we are expected to write these stories. I looked over the wire service clips on the actual story. I made a few phone calls to the town in Michigan where it occurred. The Barfman wanted it set in Boise, but I was going to stay with Michigan. I talked with the head of the public works department and a couple others. I piddled around trying to come up with a lead as it might be written by Stephen King.

Strange, unexplained forces have sent a community in Michigan spiralling out of control with fits of fear and near panic. Trees have declared war on the local population.

The nation's top scientists have been called in to try to identify the monstrous force that has tranformed harmless elms and maples into fiendish terrorists that have destroyed streets, sidewalks and lawns as well as causing thousands of dollars worth of damage to cars and trucks.

It was a start. Sometime during the day I finished it. I forget what I wrote. My eyes become as glazed as donuts after about two hours staring at the computer terminal. I can't be responsible for what I write after that. The Barfman tells me that is when I produce my best work. Only he could tell.

I spent the next part of the afternoon back in the library going through the Elvis files and drinking Shelly Bubblefarb's coffee. I learned a lot of Elvisiana. Like there are 76 independent national and international Elvis fan clubs, including the "King of Our Hearts Elvis Presley Fan Club" in San Jose, California. There were other interesting bits. Edward Asner made his film debut in Elvis' movie *Kid Galahad*; Elvis had two RCA color TVs mounted in the ceiling of his bedroom at Graceland; he was paid $50,000 for three appearances on the Ed Sullivan Show; he owned 37 guns, rifles and machine guns and was known to shoot his TV when either Robert Goulet or Mel Torme appeared on the screen; he was reading a book about the Shroud of Turin at the time of his death; and his last prescription was 50 4mg tablets of Dilaudid, 20cc-2mg solution of the same, 150 300mg quaaludes, 100

5mg tablets of Dexedrine and assorted quantities and dosages of Percodan, Amytal and Biphetamine.

It was more than most people want to know about Elvis. But not the 20 million readers of the weekly tabloids. In the two hours I browsed the files I found not one word about Jimmy Carter, the CIA or James Earl Ray.

I left the *COMET* before four p.m. in the hopes of beating the rush hour freeway traffic and Sherman Bolivia. I saw him roaming around the news room looking for someone to ambush with his jokes. Everyone had their own system to avoid Sherm. If the eye contact bit didn't work, people would go to level two. Level two ranged from jumping out of a chair—sometimes from a deep daydream—and rushing to the bathroom, the library or payroll office on urgent life-or-death business to quietly putting on the earplugs of a Sony Walkman and turning up the volume so that the only thing you could hear was your own brain disintegrating.

Sue Braska was the only person he never tried to tell his jokes to. He used to tell her jokes, until she started coming right back at him with her own jokes which would always be about fat, bald, middle-aged mediocre journalists who were sexually impotent. He stopped telling jokes to her years ago.

I got on the Hollywood Freeway going downtown where I picked up the Pasadena Freeway south to the San Diego Freeway and backtracked to the west side of Gardena. It took about as much time as it did to fill one of Elvis' mega-prescriptions.

The Cuppa Java is a small stucco cafe that is shaped like a coffee cup. The parking lot is painted to look like a saucer. Coates was inside smoking a cigarette at a booth. A cup of coffee and two donuts sat on the table in front of him. I slid into the booth opposite him.

"You got the money?" he said impatiently before I came to a full stop.

I patted my breast pocket. "In here."

"Let's have it." Coates looked exactly like he did

yesterday. His stubble had grown older and his eyes were redder, but his suit and mood were the same.

"Let's talk first." I said.

"Seven hundred dollars doesn't buy much these days, Toast. This isn't the 1950s."

I looked at him and then looked around the Cuppa Java. I could have said something smart, but didn't. "That's all my editor gave me. There may be more, but I can't guarantee it. He left the building before I could talk to him about it. Depends on what you've got to sell."

"You people are fucking with my life," he said between clenched teeth.

"Hey, don't take it personally. The *COMET* fucks with everybody's life."

Coates smirked. "Still the smart ass, eh?"

"No. I'm just a hack who works for a gutter tabloid. If I was a smart ass I'd be in an overseas bureau of the New York *Times*."

"You going to give me the dough, or what?"

I took the envelope out of my pocket and laid it on the table. "You tell me something good and it's all yours."

Coates looked at the envelope. "A lousy $700. Just enough to keep me a moving target for the Company assassins. You saw what happened to Lukins."

"Who's Lukins?"

"The Carter adviser. The CIA popped him."

"The news said it was an auto accident."

"I talked with him last week. I wanted to set up a meeting. I named a place, but he couldn't make it. You want to know why? He didn't know how to drive."

"So? He could have been a passenger."

"He was alone in the car. He was killed because he talked to me."

"What did he say?"

"Nothing. He was scared shitless. He didn't want to talk to me, but I was getting to him. I would have talked to him sooner or later. The boys in the wet operations at the Company weren't taking any chances.

45

They smoked him on the Ventura Freeway. The only reason they haven't got me yet is because I'm on to them. I'm one step ahead of Javert and his gang. But that step is getting smaller and smaller. This $700 won't even pay for my funeral."

"Like I said, there might be more. You feed me a nice big meat loaf and I'll go to bat for you with my editor."

Coates stuffed the last half of a donut into his mouth and then nervously ran his fingers through his hair. "Don't have much choice, do I?" I shrugged my shoulders.

He took a gulp of coffee to wash down the donut and calm his nerves. "Okay, I'll tell you the part about the plot against Carter."

I took out my microcorder and set it on the table. I looked at him. "Do you mind?"

"Good," he said. "Let's get it down on tape."

I pushed the record button. "Any time you're ready."

"To really understand this, you've got to know the political context of the Carter presidency. Carter gets elected in '76, right? The country is still in shock from the fall of Saigon and the defeat of its twenty-year involvement in Vietnam. That's one thing. Then there was Watergate and the disgraceful fall of an American president. That's two. Finally, there is the CIA. They were in up to their necks in both the Vietnam and Watergate disasters. And they've got their own internal problems. Those Senate investigations tore its heart out. Or tried to. They got caught with their hands in the cookie jar all over the world. Assassinations, sabotage, terrorist activities. The coup in Chile was laid right at their feet. And there were the domestic operations as well. A director was forced to resign and morale was at an all time low. This was the period when the Falcon and Snowman spy scandal breaks. American freelancers caught selling CIA cryptographic codes to the Russkies.

"Then along comes this peanut farmer from

Georgia. People want to break with the failures of the Vietnam-CIA-Nixon past. What is the first thing he does as President? He fires the CIA director. Who is the director? George Bush. He picks Ted Sorenson to replace him. A Kennedy liberal to be CIA director! Alarm bells go off. It's a death sentence to the old hands in the Company. Ted Shackley, 'The Blond Ghost', Mr. Clandestine Operations himself, resigns. With him go the Edwin Wilsons, the Tom Clines and the James Angletons. Shackley and Clines become major players as independents and pop up in Iran-Contra ten years later.

"The opposition is so great that Carter backs down and withdraws the Sorenson nomination. But he doesn't back down on his foreign policy. Carter has his own ideas about Angola and Panama. Big problem for the Company. In Angola, Carter refuses to support the CIA-backed war against the Marxists. The Cubans send in troops to help the Angolans. Carter's ambassador to the UN is Andrew Young. A frigging civil rights activist. Maybe a communist as far as the hardliners in the Company are concerned. Young tells the world that the Cuban troops are a 'stabilizing force' in Angola. Can you dig it? The Company is left to twist in the wind. Carter has scrambled all the eggs in the CIA's southern Africa basket.

"Then comes Panama. A US-CIA outpost in Central America. Carter negotiates a treaty with the Marxist Torrijo government to turn the Canal over to Panama in the year 2000. Even some of the moderates screamed bloody sellout. The CIA was betrayed again. Carter had undercut its efforts to prop up Somoza in Nicaragua against the Sandinista guerrillas who were building up their strength.

"Then a curious thing happens. This is in May 1977. General John Singlaub. Remember him? He and Secord were the money men in Iran-Contra. Well, in 1977 Singlaub was chief of staff of US military forces in Korea. On May 22, he was reprimanded and demoted for criticizing Carter's public pledge to withdraw

American ground troops from Korea. From that date Singlaub goes into the underground opposition. This is the guy who is the head of the ultra right-wing World Anti-Communist League. Three years later he is in Central America supplying the death squad governments of Guatemala and El Salvador with 'counter-terror' training.

"Carter did other things to put the noose around his neck. Like opening a diplomatic front to Cuba. The anti-Castroites in Miami went apeshit. In April of '77 Carter signed a fishing rights treaty with Castro. By June they were exchanging diplomats. By that time Carter was marked for death the same way JFK was. The word was out in certain circles that Carter had to go. Like feet first."

"What circles?" I asked.

"The circles that have been running American foreign policy since the Eisenhower years. Cowboy elements in the CIA, the anti-Castro Cubans they had created into a fighting terrorist force and certain military brass hats like Secord and Singlaub who are fanatical anti-communists and moonlight as weapons and drug traffickers.

"These are the guys who brought you the Bay of Pigs, the Kennedy assassination, the Phoenix program in Vietnam, the drug trade from Laos, Ollie North and the Iran-Contra mess. A sweet bunch, don't you think?"

I had to admit I was impressed with the man's lucidness. Especially for a person who appeared to exist on coffee, donuts and little sleep. Names, dates, connections, they were all there, but only in the most superficial way. I asked him for some evidence.

"Evidence?" he said, as if I had just called him a name.

"Yeah. Like evidence that all these guys got together and actually plotted to kill the President."

"A lot of it died last night on the Ventura Freeway."

"I was afraid you were going to say that."

"To hell with you! Lukins was my smoking gun, but I don't need him to bust this wide open."

"What do you need?"

"I need a smart ass rag peddler to take me seriously and print my story."

"Go on, then."

"The plan to hit Carter came together just after Singlaub got kicked downstairs, but it had been on the drawing boards since the day after the '76 election. In fact, a group of the conspirators met at Toots Shor's restaurant in New York in early January of '77. Two anti-Castro Cubans were dining with Buckley Bergeron. Bergeron was a former station chief for the Company in Panama. The Cubans were vets of the Bay of Pigs."

"How do you know all of this?" I interrupted.

"They were seen and identified by Herbert Matthews, the famous correspondent for the New York *Times*. He was an expert on Cuba. He was in the hills with Castro in '58, writing about the revolution. He knew all of them from the Bay of Pigs. Matthews let other people know what he saw. That's how I know who was there."

"No, I mean the whole thing. How did you get this information about Elvis and the CIA?"

Coates shifted in his seat. He was uncomfortable with the question. "What's the difference? I got it, that's what counts. Go ahead, check out what I'm telling you. You'll find I'm on the level."

"I just want to know where you got this stuff. Are you ex-CIA?"

"You want to hear this story or sit here cross-examining me on my bona fides?" Coates was angry. I thought I might be about to lose him.

"You were saying Herbert Matthews was at Toots Shor's."

"Freddie Prinze was there, too."

"The comedian who blew his brains out?"

"That's what they'd like you to believe."

"What are you talking about?"

"I had a friend who was a waiter at Shor's. He's been in hiding more than ten years. Probably dead by now. I haven't seen him since '79. He was working that night. He told me the Cubans had too much to drink and began shooting off their mouths about blowing away the supporters of the Cuban revolution and taking back the island. They talked freely about their hatred for Carter. Toots Shor spent time at their table. So did Freddie Prinze. The Cubans, it seems, were big fans of *Chico and the Man* and invited him to have a few drinks with them. Matthews was sitting at a nearby table and must have heard a lot of what was being said by Bergeron and the Cubans."

"So did probably dozens of others."

"Yeah, but they didn't end up dead."

I wrinkled my nose and looked annoyed. "Prinze committed suicide. There was never any doubt raised."

"Exactly. Were any doubts raised about Toots Shor's death? Or Herbert Matthews'? Shor died one week after that January dinner meeting. Matthews passed away on July 30, just two weeks before Elvis Presley's so-called drug overdose."

"Are you trying to tell me all those people were killed because they heard a couple of drunk Cubans make some idle threats about killing the President?"

"They may have heard a lot more than drunken threats. We will never know for sure."

"Coincidence. People have to die sometime. Matthews and Shor were old men."

"Freddie Prinze was 22. And what about the others around the conspiracy who died mysteriously? They were all ages. You think it was just coincidence?"

"But what about the plot. You haven't told me a thing about any conspiracy to kill the preseident. Three guys having dinner at Toots Shor's is hardly a CIA murder plot."

"Fred Cowan, David Berkowitz, Johnny Nebiscio and Roscoe Poteet. They were the Rebounders."

"The Rebounders? Sounds like a basketball team."

Coates smiled and took a gulp of cold coffee. "The meter just ran out, Toast. You want any more, you've got to come up with the cash. And I don't mean another lousy $700."

"How much are we talking about?"

"You want the rest of the story, it's going to cost you five grand."

Coates got up from the booth and walked out of the Cuppa Java without saying another word. I would have called after him, but I knew he would contact me. He had me where he wanted me—wanting more.

I didn't know what to think. Maybe there wasn't any more. Maybe this was all a con job. Maybe it was an excuse for Coates to tour the coffee joints of greater Los Angeles. Maybe he was writing a guide book to bad coffee and jelly donuts and had suckered the *COMET* into bankrolling it. I just didn't know. He was truly a mystery wrapped in an enigma inside a riddle who wanted $5,000 to either pick the *COMET*'s pocket clean or serve up the biggest story since the Kennedy assassination.

I took Sepulveda back to Venice. I caught the first few innings of the Dodgers-Cubs game on the radio. I had half a notion to drive out to Chavez to catch the rest of it, but I didn't. For me, going to a baseball game is the same as going to a movie. If I can't make it in time for the first pitch or the opening credits, I don't go. Even if the score is nothing-to-nothing, which it was.

I thought I picked up a tail near El Segundo. A big, fast Mercury stayed with me until I turned off the boulevard. I turned the corner and headed to Ralph's to pick up my dinner. I told myself I was becoming paranoid.

I varied my menu by replacing the potato salad with a macaroni and pimento number. A large bag of Dorito chips complemented my pickle and roast beef with mayo on onion roll. Two large bottles of soda water and an apple completed my shopping.

I was less than a mile from home. In LA that is almost like being there. I had the Dodgers on the radio, my dinner in a bag on the seat next to me and the smell of the ocean up my nose. Life was good. That is until I looked in my rearview mirror. The big, fast Mercury was back.

I raced up Lincoln Boulevard in an effort to ditch him. I cut off another big, fast car trying to make a light. I sped through Venice and turned onto Pico. Both cars were now in pursuit. My rearview mirror was made useless by the golden glint of the setting sun as I headed east on Pico. I couldn't tell which car was which.

My Datsun was no match for the multiple tons of fast, angry metal and rubber in hot pursuit. They began to pull up along either side of me. I was approaching a wide and very busy intersection. I thought if I could cut a sharp right turn, they would slide into the cross streets. That would slow them down.

Just as I went into a breaking slide and turn I heard a gunshot. Or rather, gunshots. I heard at least two. I knew they were shots because one of them came through the open window on the driver's side of my car and plowed into my dinner bag. The slug shattered my bottles of soda water.

I made the turn and sped down a side street. I snaked down a few more streets before working my way back to Lincoln Boulevard. I looked in my rearview mirror. Nothing but the approaching night. I had lost them. I took a deep breath at a stop light. I was alive, but life was not good anymore. Some people I didn't know had just tried to kill me.

Chapter 8

This was getting much too serious. And dangerous. I was paid to talk to all kinds of head cases and eccentrics, but they didn't pay me to get shot at.

I could have called the cops, but that would have been a waste of everybody's time. There are several top-notch private investigation firms that will look into things for $300 a day. I could just see handing the Barfman an expense voucher for a couple days services from a corporate PI firm. Besides, I wasn't sure $300 a day could tell me what I wanted to know. That's why I went to see Marty Angelo.

Marty Angelo was more of a snitch than a private detective. He had big ears and when the money was up front, an even bigger mouth. He sold rumors, some drugs and the confidences of people who were outbid in the market place. To a lot of people who knew him, Marty Angelo was a guy who gave sleaze a bad name.

But he was thorough. He freelanced information to the *COMET* for years. And it was always pretty reliable. As reliable as any of the stuff that appears in the *COMET* can be called reliable. And he was certainly cheaper than the high rent PIs with their electronic surveillance devices. I figured I could get something out of him for fifty bucks. That much I could afford myself. I mean, after all, I had just been shot at.

Marty Angelo lived in a trailer on the Coast

Highway just across the Venice city line. His address in the phone book was Marina Del Rey. It was a much classier address and Marty knew it. "It gets the not-sures who are turned off by Venice," he once told me. "If I can get them out here and through the front door I can gill net 'em and haul 'em aboard nine times out of ten." Marty Angelo cared about people.

I parked in the lot of Ramona's Clam House and Lounge. Angelo's trailer squatted just beyond the far end of the pavement. I walked up to his door and knocked. And knocked. I looked around. The last time I saw him he was driving an old blue Impala. I saw it conspicuously parked thirty feet from the trailer.

I banged on the door. "Open up, Marty. I know you're in there. It's me, Steve Toast."

I heard the clatter clack of metal door bolts and chains. The door opened an inch. An eyeball took a chance on my story. I stared back at it. The door closed, then swung open and a hand shot out and grabbed me by the arm and dragged me inside.

"God, am I glad to see you, Steve," Marty Angelo said, with all the sincerity of a utility bill. He shut the door and began throwing bolts and turning latches like they were instruments to the flight panel of a commercial airliner.

"Who is it this time, Marty? The cops? Sharks? The IRS? Or did another con go west on you?"

"No, nothing like that. Why do you always have to think the worst of people?"

"In your case, Marty, it comes with knowing you. You're as predictable as yesterday's weather."

"There's two guys out there who want to give me the Roselli-in-a-drum treatment and I have to stand here and take this verbal abuse in my own home? What kind of friend are you, Toast?"

"What two guys?"

"Never mind. It's a long story."

"Marty! What two guys? Did you run one of your harebrained scams on the mafia?"

"Harebrained?" Angelo shouted. He went over to a

54

window and pulled the drawn shade aside a half-inch. He then turned to me. "Harebrained? You should have seen it, Steve. It was brilliant. A real masterpiece."

"If it was a masterpiece how come you are holed up here like Butch Cassidy?"

Marty dropped his head into his chest. "I'll admit a few snags developed," he said sheepishly. "But they could have been ironed out. In principle, it was a gem."

"What was it, Marty? You try to sell them land in Griffith Park?"

"I took the red barn con to new heights." He sounded so proud of himself.

"And now the marks want to take you to new depths, right?"

Marty shrugged and lit a cigarette. He started to say something, but nothing he could say to me would get him out of the jam he was in and he knew it.

He started to say something again. This time he succeeded. "Steve, my man. Can you float your old pard a small loan?"

"How small?"

"Just a couple of yards."

"I can go fifty."

"I need at least a hundred."

"A hundred?"

"It'll buy me a few days at my sister's place in the Valley until this thing blows over."

"You have to pay to stay with your sister?"

Marty Angelo looked away. "We ain't been on such good terms since...." His voice trailed off.

"Since you tried to sell her house without telling her. I remember that one."

"I thought she was in the Bahamas. I swear, I wasn't really going to sell it. The plan was to get the down and then back out of the deal. You know Night Court Billy Boyer, don't you?" I nodded. "He used to be a lawyer before he got disbarred. Anyway, he said he'd run this con a dozen times and it was foolproof."

"Marty. What do you think got Billy Boyer disbarred?"

"I don't know. What am I, his biographer? We were partners, that's all." He paused. A light went on in his head. "Oh, yeah, well." The words escaped from his mouth like air from a punctured tire.

"That's right. Real estate fraud."

"Well, it would have worked, but Nancy came back early and queered the whole deal. I was going to cut her in. I had her down for ten percent."

"I'm surprised she will let you stay at her place at all."

"You should see the rent she charges me. She thinks she's Howard Johnson or somebody." Angelo held his hand out. "I'll take that 'C' note, now, Steve. You're a real buddy. Mainday!" He made his hand into a fist and pounded the air as a signal of approval.

"Hold on, Marty. I'm not just going to give you a hundred dollars."

The expression on Marty Angelo's face dropped like an elevator with a snapped cable. "I knew it," he huffed. "I knew there would be strings attached. There usually is when ol' Marty is in a jam. Only those strings turn out to be ropes. Hanging ropes. And I'm just not ready to die. I thought you was my friend, Steve," He hung his head and went into an act of feeling betrayed. I ignored it. It was a bad act.

"I want to hire you to do a job."

He snapped his head to attention and looked at me suspiciously. "What kind of job?"

"I want you to check out a guy for me."

"Sure, no problem. What's his name?"

"Hang on. Someone in a big grey Mercury took some shots at me less than an hour ago."

"Uh, uh, Steve. When I hear the word 'shots', the price goes up."

"The price isn't going up, Marty. It's a hundred bucks with or without the shots."

"I'm no hero. Who do you think I am, Chuck Morris?"

"No, you're a man who needs a hundred bucks to get out from under yet another chuckleheaded con. And

56

it's Norris, not Morris. You want the hundred or not?"

"You got the cash on you? Marty Angelo don't do no credit banking. Cash-and-dash. That's where I'm coming from."

I took out my wallet and pulled out two twenties and a ten. "Half now and the rest when I get the information I want."

Marty scowled and grabbed the money from my hand. "I'm real disappointed in you, Steve. I thought we was friends. I thought we could trust each other. You know I'm good for the whole hundred."

"I'm not even sure about the fifty, but neither one of us has much choice."

"Real disappointed."

I spent the next ten minutes telling him about Coates and his paranoia about the CIA. I told him to see what he could find out about him and to stake out my next meeting with him and look for big grey Mercuries. I wanted to know what the connection was between Coates and Mercuries taking shots at me. I told Marty I expected a license plate number. He agreed to everything. Whether he would do any of it was another question entirely.

As soon as he got the fifty from me he was in a big hurry to clear out of his trailer. He wanted to give me some of his clothes. Just in case anything happened to him, he said. He gave me one of his best jackets and his favorite hat. I told him it was unnecessary and he would live to run another scam, but he insisted. He said he wanted me to have his things. I accepted them, but when I refused to put them on and wear them out of the trailer and trade cars with him, he got indignant and took everything back. Marty Angelo was a guy who could have used a friend. Or a perfect stranger, for that matter.

Chapter 9

I marched into the Barfman's office the first thing the next day. He was surprised. Few staff writers come to see him unless they are summoned.

"Coates wants more money," I said. "I say we give it to him."

The Barfman was reading the galleys for next week's *COMET*. He was only paying half attention to me. "How much does he want?" he said, nonchalantly.

"Five thousand."

"Five thousand!" The *COMET* editor dropped the galleys and looked me in the eye like I was crazy. "Are you crazy?" he yelped.

"Actually, the way I figure it, it is only forty-three hundred. I gave him seven yesterday."

"Only forty-three hundred," he said, mockingly. "What do you think the *COMET* is? The goddamn lottery payout office?"

"Someone tried to kill me last night."

"I wouldn't pay forty-three hundred if Elvis' corpse were wheeled in here on a block of ice. It may come as a complete surprise to you, Toast, but we try to make money at this newspaper, not go out of our way to lose it." He stopped abruptly. "What did you say?"

"I said someone tried to kill me last night. Took a shot at me as I was driving home."

"A drive-by?"

"I don't think so."

"Are you sure? Drive-by shootings have replaced racquetball and sailing as the leading recreational activity in LA."

"Someone followed me from my meeting with Coates."

"And they shot at you?"

"I think so. There was a second car involved."

"Two of them? Christ, Toast, I knew you had enemies, but a double drive-by." The Barfman snapped his fingers. "Say, why not write it up? It would make a great page three lead. I can see the head—'Turbo Charged Terrorists Stalk the Streets of Urban America.'"

"That's just great. I have become my own trashy tabloid story."

"Yeah. Tell you what. You take the rest of the morning to work on it. I'll talk to accounting. We can probably get you an extra hundred dollars out of the victims fund. Yeah, I like it, Toast."

"Well, that makes one of you. Are you going to pony up more money for Coates or not?"

"Coates? Who the hell—"

"Deep Coates. You remember? The guy who is going to send the *COMET*'s circulation into orbit and make us all rich and famous."

"Oh, yeah, sure."

"Oh, yeah, sure, what?"

"How much does he want again?"

"Forty-three hundred."

"Jesus Hubert Christ in a Nehru jacket! Give him a grand and tell him to stuff it."

"What if he won't give me the whole story?"

"What have you got so far?"

I took out my microcorder and played the first twenty minutes.

The Barfman got that dreamy, far away look in his eyes again. He was tripping on lurid headlines and circulation surges.

I leaned over his desk. "Los Angeles calling Stan

Barfyskowicz."

"Yeah, yeah. Forty-three hundred, you said. Give the bastard two thousand and tell him to lump it or dump it. But whatever you do, don't let the sonofabitch walk away. We need that story, Toast. You hear me? We need that story! I'm thinking six-part series. That would really jump us over the *SUN*. Make sure our Deep Coates hasn't cut a deal with the SUN or any of the other rags. If they get wind of this they will outbid us sure as my grandmother wears combat boots."

"She does?"

"Does what?"

"Wear combat boots."

"Who?"

"Your grandmother."

"What about my grandmother?"

"Skip it."

"You're a dingaling, Toast, you know that?"

"Yeah."

"Okay, now beat it. I've got to finish with next week's galleys. You can draw the money from Accounting." Barfyskowicz ripped a page from his note pad, wrote in the amount and signed it. He handed it to me. "This is a lot of money, Toast. The *COMET* is counting on you. Don't screw up!"

"Thanks, chief." The Barfman was back looking over the galleys before I turned to leave his office. "Don't screw up," he told me. Not "don't get hurt," or "don't get shot." It was "don't screw up." That was the *COMET*'s motto— "don't screw up."

I went back into the news room. Sherm Bolivia and Sue City Braska were sitting at their desks. Sue was filing a story at her computer terminal. Sherm was eating a pound cake.

"Sherm," I said, walking over to his desk. He quickly wrapped up the remains of the cake and shoved it into a drawer. "What?" he said, tersely. "I'm busy."

I pulled a nearby chair up to his desk and sat down. "You know a lot about Elvis, right?"

"Only about all there is to know, that's all. I've

been covering Elvis for more than twenty years. The man lives in my heart."

"Then he must have died of cholesterol poisoning," said Sue from the other side of the shoulder-high office divider that separated her desk from Sherm's. I could hear the clicking of her keyboard. Sue was the kind of person who could carry on a conversation and sometimes an argument while filing a story. And she could do it without misspelling a word.

"This is a private conversation, Ms. Braska," said Sherm, coldly. "We will thank you to keep your trap shut."

"In your hairy ears, Sherman."

Sherm leaned over toward me. "Ignore her, Toast. Now, what is it you want to know about Elvis?"

"Do you think there is a possibility—even a remote possibility—that Elvis was murdered?"

"Sure, there is a possibility. With all the screwups around the autopsy and the burial, anything could have happened. Personally, I don't buy it, but if I did, I'd put twenty bucks on the nose of Dr. Nick."

"Who's that?"

Sherm shook his head. "Boy, you don't know anything, do you, Toast? Dr. George Nichopoulos, Elvis' personal doctor. He wrote him prescriptions for a ton of pills. Elvis took them all. Uppers, downers, Dilaudid, Dexedrine, Amytal. Everything. Elvis never met a pill he didn't like. Anyway, some people think Dr. Nick pushed Elvis into taking an overdose. Why? Who knows? Maybe it was because borrowed 250 thousand big ones from Elvis and couldn't pay it back. I'm not accusing anybody, but there has been talk."

"Sherm belongs to the Geraldo Rivera school of journalism," said Sue City, again without dropping the cadence from her clacking keyboard.

"You should be so lucky, missus," said Sherm, rising halfway up from his chair. "In fact, Toast, it was Geraldo who uncovered the cover-up on '20-20'. He found, one, there was no police investigation into Elvis' death; two, the contents of Elvis' stomach were

61

destroyed without ever being analyzed; three, all photos taken at the death scene, all the notes of the Medical Examiner's investigation and all of the toxicology reports allegedly prepared by the ME were missing from the official files; four—"

"Whoa, Sherm, I just asked about the possibility of murder, not the Warren Report."

"I told you, Toast, I know all there is to know about Elvis."

"You know all there is to know about sleaze, too," said Sue. "Don't forget to take credit for that, too, Bolivia."

Sherm looked a little embarrassed. It was more from the interruptions than Sue's nasty comments. He made an obscene gesture at the office divider.

"Sherm," I said. "This may sound crazy, but do you think the CIA could have had anything to do with Elvis' death?"

"The CIA? Are you nuts! I thought you stopped reading those left-wing skin mags about conspiracy crap. Still jerkin' your gherkin over capitalist-imperialist plots? You people make me laugh, Toast."

"Hey, I'm just asking."

"Skin mags and gherkins," said Sue. "Some other things about which Sherman knows everything there is know."

"Bitch!"

"No, really, you guys. I'm serious."

"Then," quipped Sue," you're talking to the wrong people, at the wrong newspaper in the wrong city." Sue City was something of a cynic.

I got up from my chair and walked to the office partition. I rested my elbows along the top and looked down at her. "What do you think, Sue? You've written about Elvis in your time. Do you think the CIA could have had anything to do with his death?"

Sue didn't look up from her keyboard. She types eighty words a minutes. It looked more like one hundred-and-eighty. It was so effortless for her. Like she was sewing a quilt. "Just between you and me, honey," she said, "when it comes to the CIA, I believe everything I hear. I mean everything. Nothing those pricks do would surprise me anymore."

"Don't listen to the ignorant opinions from an uninformed person," Sherm said to my back. "The CIA did not kill Elvis Presley. Take it from a man who is an expert on the subject." He raised his voice. "Are you an expert on Elvis Presley, missus? No, you are not."

"The only thing I'm an expert on these days, is writing dreck. I haven't been sitting next to the dreckmeister himself all these years for nothing. You want dreck, I know dreck. Look it up in the dictionary and you'll find my picture."

"Forget her, Toast. She's having hot flashes again. It happens to women when they get to her age. Just drop this bullshit about the CIA. You want to know anything else, okay. I'm your boy."

"Sherman," Sue countered. "You were never a boy. You were born fat, bald and fifty."

Sherm rolled his chair over to me and poked me in the back. I turned around. "Menopause," he whispered. "It makes 'em bitchy as the nuns in a Catholic grade school."

"I heard that, Bolivia. You want bitchy, I'll show you bitchy, you wiener."

"Say, Toast, did I ever tell you the one about the priest, the minister and the rabbi?"

I turned slowly and just walked away. Sherm and Sue were still mixing it up. I could hear them. I stopped and looked back. I could see Sue at her terminal punching out words on her keyboard. Sherm had taken the rest of his pound cake out of his desk and was stuffing his face. Sometimes they carried on their name-calling for hours without ever laying eyes on one another. It was something else they were both experts at.

Chapter 10

I sat at my desk waiting for the phone call from Coates. I killed time listlessly going over my story assignments like they were magazines in a dentist's office. There was a note from the Barfman urging me to write up my "double drive-by," as he called it. The man was serious.

The call came before I did anything rash, like actually writing up my escapade in Venice. Coates sounded more panicked than ever. He appeared to be hyperventilating. He said he was leaving town on an afternoon train. He told me to meet him at a beanery in West Covina in an hour. He told me to bring cash money and make sure I wasn't being followed. Then he hung up.

I called Marty Angelo and told him when and where I was meeting Coates. He told me he had another appointment and couldn't make it. I told him to break it if he wanted to see the other fifty bucks or ever sell anything to the *COMET* again. Marty Angelo always responded well to threats.

I went to the accounting department and got the money. I asked for cash, but didn't get it. Nobody in this country has cash anymore. Businesses, gas stations, bakery truck drivers—no one. It must take a significant bite out of the armed robbery trade. Lucky for me the banks still carried money. I cashed the draft and jumped in my car.

I took the Ventura Freeway through Pasadena all the way to Duarte where I picked up the San Gabriel going south. I jumped over to the San Bernardino at El Monte. From there it was a breeze into West Covina. Thirty-five miles, it was. In New England I would have been in another state. But this is Los Angeles where traveling over vast wasteland to reach the extremities of nowhere is an everyday thing. Sort of like breathing the air.

I like driving. All Angelinos like driving. You pretty much have to if you live here. LA is a place where when you go out for a walk you take your car. It is a cultural thing as well as a transportational imperative. A British scholar came to Los Angeles several years ago to write a book about Southland architecture. He did not drive in his native London, but learned immediately upon arriving here. "I wanted to be able to speak American in the original," he said.

It took less than an hour to get to Covina and another fifteen minutes looking for Ramona's Diner. It was a railroad dining car that had seen better days. Better years.

Coates was sitting in the last booth at the rear of the long, narrow cafe. His coffee was in a pink crockery mug and his donuts were stacked on a small paper plate. I ordered a cup of coffee on my way to join him. The waitress was a bleached blonde on the bad side of fifty. The cubic yard of make-up on her face didn't help any. Her hair was tucked under an old-fashion white waitress cap. Her white uniform dress had lost a lot of its starch. She and the diner seemed to be a set. A set from the 1940s.

I took my coffee to Coates' booth. "Give me the cash," he said. "I'm in a hurry. I'm going over to my place after this to get a few things then I'm blowing this town. I don't know when I will be back. Maybe never." He looked at his watch. "My train leaves in two hours."

"If you're in such a rush, why take the train? A plane, it should go without saying, is considerably

65

faster."

"Haven't you learned anything? The CIA controls the major airlines. Probably the smaller ones, too. I would be walking right into their hands. I wouldn't have a chance. Were you on another planet when Korean Airlines 007 went down in '83?"

"Okay, okay. I should've known."

"You got the money, or what?"

"I've got two thousand. That's all I could get."

"Give it to me." Coates' bloodshot eyes twitched with impatience. "You can owe me the rest."

"There isn't any 'rest'."

"Give it to me, anyway." He nearly leaped across the table. "I've got to blow this town. Today! You understand that, Toast? Javert is closing in. You're talking to a dead man."

It isn't that I don't have a heart. It's just that I've heard all the hardluck stories before. Killer husbands on the loose; killer diseases; killer bees. I've met a lot of desperate people in my line of work who tell me a lot of desperate stories, most of them false. They believe them, but what they tell me just doesn't always fit the facts very well. But what the hell, it wasn't my money. If it was up to me, I would have given him the two grand and bought him another round of coffee and donuts out of my own pocket. I guess that's what the Barfman meant when he said, "Don't screw up."

"You've got something to sell?" I said, taking out my microcorder and setting it on the table. "Yesterday you fed me the weight-watcher's lunch. Today, I want a hot roast beef sandwich smothered with gravy and a double order of mashed potatoes."

"Okay, okay," he said, pointing at my tiny tape recorder. "Turn it on so we can get this over with." I pressed the record button.

"You remember where you left off?" I asked.

"Yeah, yeah. I gave you the names of the Rebounders, right?"

"The basketball guys."

"Screw that! Operation Rebound. That was the hit

66

squad's code name. I mean this was deep, deep cover stuff. Stansfield Turner didn't know squat about it. A lot of others didn't, either. This was Secret Team business. The Rebounders were the trigger men. Total whackos when you look into their backgrounds. I'm pretty sure they were psychologically programmed, but I can't quite prove it, yet."

"Tell me something about them."

"If I had all day I could give you their complete stinking biographies. What's important to know is the chain of command. I mean from Shackley, North, Singlaub and Secord and the rest right down to the actual trigger men. It's a fairly direct line. You don't need to know the team leaders' motives, do you? Unless you were on a life support system during the Iranscam hearings you know who those guys are and how they operate and even why. What we need to know here is the link between the brains and the gunslingers. The operational guys were the link. They ran the gunslingers and reported upstairs to the team leaders."

"So, who were the operational people?"

"I already told you."

"You told me about the Rebounders."

"Remember that dinner at Toots Shor's?"

"Ah."

"Operations was run by Bergeron and the two Cubans— Jesus Obledo and Gonzalez Petrakis."

"And these Rebounders. Who were they?"

"Basically, there were four. Four that I know about. You've got Johnny 'Crackers' Nebiscio. He was a career hitman. Did a lot of free-lancing for the Gambino crime family. He was the key player in the plot to assassinate Carter. I'll tell you more about him later.

"The others were Roscoe Poteet, Fred Cowan and David Berkowitz. Poteet was most likely the one picked to be the main trigger. He was a career criminal. His best asset was that he was black. The team leaders wanted a black man to kill Carter. That would throw everyone off the trail. You know, lone black nut who hated peckerwoods. Even kind, sympathetic peckerwoods like Jimmy Carter.

"Next is Fred Cowan. He was the one who led me to believe the others were neurologically programmed. Cowan was a Vietnam vet who went berserk in February of '77. He went on a shooting spree in New York. He killed five people before he turned the rifle on himself. I was in New York at the time and followed the incident because something smelled fishy about it. I tracked down some leads that directed me to a CIA operation in Vietnam that brought him and Bergeron together. Later, Cowan turned up working for the U.S. Embassy in Panama. I think the whole plot was hatched there. There is a little-known Army psychological testing center in the Canal Zone. Like the MK-ULTRA mind control operation that was exposed about ten years ago.

"The fourth guy on the team is David Berkowitz. You might know him better as 'Son of Sam'."

"Oh, get out of here!" I blurted out, involuntarily.

"Hey, this is what went down. I'm just the guy who put two and two together."

"Are you trying to tell me that David Berkowitz was programmed by the CIA to assassinate Jimmy Carter?"

"Where do you think those voices that told him to kill came from?"

"Didn't he say it was his dog?"

"His dog? Listen to yourself. Who's the crazy one here?" I dipped my head and shrugged my shoulders. "I think what happened was that Cowan and Berkowitz got short circuits in their wires and malfunctioned. I can quote you chapter and verse where it has happened before.

"There was one more player in the game I didn't tell you about. He came after the Rebounders began blowing fuses all over the place. He was sent to do a plumbing job. He was the Company's man on the inside."

"Inside of what?"

"Inside Elvis' circle. He was an AKA artist. A man

68

of a thousand names and disguises. He was sometimes known as Dr. Chaim Gershowitz. I also know him as Benny 'The Mixmaster' Daniels. Problem is, I don't know his name when he was working for Elvis. But he was a chemist. Toxicology was his specialty. That's a polite way to say he manufactured drugs. Since I've never been able to find a picture of him I don't know what he looks like. My bet is he worked for Elvis in some capacity other than a doctor or pharmacist. That would have been too easy to track him down. But one thing is sure, Benny could mix up any number of deadly combinations of pills."

"So, what does he have to do with the plot against Carter?"

"None. Listen to what I'm telling you, Toast. He was sent to plug up the leaks when the Rebound operation began to spring leaks. When Elvis learned the Company was planning to hit the president, the team sent Benny to silence him."

My recorder ran out of tape. I put in a new cassette and pressed the record button and nodded for Coates to continue.

"This is where it all comes together. Remember Johnny Crackers? Rebound's freelance mafia hit man? Well, Johnny got mixed up with the Attorney General's office on a totally different matter. They wanted him to testify in a mafia contract case and dumped him into the witness protection program. They snatched him one night in New York and took him to Tennessee and deposited him in Brushy State Prison for safekeeping. The AG's office didn't know he was CIA and when Johnny Crackers hollered about it, they went to Turner, who, of course, knew nothing about any Johnny Crackers being in the employ of the Central Intelligence Agency. So, Johnny Crackers just sat and stewed at Brushy. You can bet he was plenty sore about it, too. He probably thought Bergeron and the team had hung him out in the shed to dry.

"Anyway, it wasn't long before he starts shooting off his mouth to anyone who will listen. Turns out he's got a neighbor who likes to listen to people shoot off their mouths."

"James Earl Ray, right?"

"You're catching up, Toast. Right, James Earl Ray. Now, Ray's got his own problems. I think he was a patsy in the King assassination, but that's another story. Anyway, Ray is no friend of Carter's liberal civil rights positions, to say the least. But they are both good ol' southern boys and ten years in stir has given Ray a lot of time to think about political assassination."

"So, Ray breaks jail."

"Right. June 10th. He got help and he had his own agenda. High on the list is to make contact with Elvis Presley and tell him about the hit on Carter."

"Why Elvis? Why not go directly to Carter?"

Coates looked at me like I had asked him who was buried in Elvis' tomb. Make that Grant's tomb. There still seems to be some doubt as to who lies beneath the marble at Graceland.

"Ray was the most famous man behind bars in America. Do you think he was just going to turkey trot into the Oval Office and have scooter pies and milk with the President of the United States of America? Get real, Toast. Even if he could have made it as far as the White House or Plains, Georgia, James Earl Ray would be the last person on earth to get in to see Carter. Well, maybe Charlie Manson would be the last, but I think you get the point. Ray knew this. Anyone with a brain would."

"Except me, that is."

"Yeah, I guess so."

"Okay, color me stupid, but I still don't see why Ray would go to Elvis Presley. Elvis wasn't exactly a political adviser to Carter."

"No, but Elvis had access to anybody on the planet. He was the king, man, and kings do what they want to do and go where they want to go."

"And that includes dropping in on the President?"

Coates looked at his watch. "Look, Toast, I'll make this short. I've got places to go. In December, 1970 Elvis

70

disappeared for a few days. No one knew where he was. He surfaced in a D.C. hotel under the name John Burrows. He met with the Deputy Director of the Bureau of Narcotics and Dangerous Drugs. He had it in his head that he wanted to be an undercover nark in the entertainment industry. He didn't like what Jane Fonda and the Smothers Brothers were doing."

"What were they doing?"

"Promoting left-wing causes and the drug culture. But that's not important. He didn't get very far at the BNDD. On impulse, he wrote a note to Nixon. The next day he's at the White House meeting with America's top man. They talked for thirty minutes. Some heads of state don't get that much time with the President. Elvis had access. Ray knew that. Besides, Elvis was an idol of his. Why not mix business with hero worship? And for another reason, Elvis was close by the prison. When you come right down to it, Elvis was the most logical person for Ray to see."

"But I thought Ray was captured in the woods right near the prison. I don't remember hearing that he contacted anyone."

"You wouldn't have known about it if he did. I have proof that Ray made contact with Elvis. It wasn't face-to-face, but there is no doubt he talked with Elvis and told him the details of the plot to kill Carter as he heard them from Johnny Crackers."

"I'd like to see your documentation."

"Don't worry, I've got it in a safe place." Coates looked at his watch again. He picked up a cream-filled maple bar and took a big bite. "Give me the dough, Toast. I've got to get out of here."

"But we're not finished. I've got a lot of questions. What about Elvis? If what you say is true, did Elvis get to Carter? Or even try?"

Coates slid to the edge of the booth. "You've just bought yourself two thousand dollars' worth of the biggest story since the Crucifixion. You got it dirt cheap. You've got enough for ten stories. A book. Give me the goddamn money!"

I took twenty one-hundred dollar bills from my wallet and passed them across the table to him. He stood up and scooped the money and stuffed it into his jacket pocket. I slid out of the booth. Coates was already leaning toward the door. He reached back for the last quarter of his maple bar before leaving.

"Where can I get in touch with you?" I asked.

"You can't." He turned and began walking to the front door.

I called after him. "Will you contact me again? I might be able to get you some more money." I got out of the booth and followed him. I was a couple of steps behind him as he reached the door.

"Too late for that, now," he said. He stopped at the door and looked out through the glass. "They're out there, Toast. I can feel them."

"Let me take you to the train station."

"Get out of my life, Toast. Just write the story and forget about me."

"But what if they really do get to you? How will I even know? I should know. It would be good for the story."

Coates stepped back from the door and looked at me for a long moment. The fear and panic in his eyes had subsided. They looked more sad than anything else. They were almost sorrowful.

"I have an aunt near here," he said. He reached into his coat pocket and took out an envelope. "Give me your pen." I handed him my pen. He wrote a phone number on the back of it and handed it to me. "If anything happens to me, call this number. Please do it. She will want to know."

"What's your aunt's name?"

Coates looked me in the eyes. "Be careful, Toast. The Company wants to kill me for what I know. Now you know what I know and they will want to kill you, too." He took a deep breath and pushed through the door.

I watched him until he turned in the parking lot and disappeared. I went to the counter and told the waitress I wanted to pay for the "murk and sinkers." She didn't know what I was talking about. If I had told her Elvis Presley was murdered by the CIA because James Earl Ray told him about the Agency plot to assassinate the President of the United States, she would have probably called the cops. I wouldn't have blamed her if she did, but I was disappointed she didn't know about murk and sinkers.

Chapter 11

I didn't return to the *COMET*. I was done for the day. Literally. I wanted to be alone. And I was hungry. So I went where hungry people eat when they want to be alone—a cafeteria. But I didn't go to any old jello and chicken wing joint. I went to Clifton's. The original Clifton's on Broadway in downtown LA.

Clifton's is a shrine to cheap meals, bad taste in wall decor and the art of being in a public place with hundreds of people, yet providing the opportunity to be totally alone if you want to. "Anonymous" may be a better word than "alone." No waiters, waitresses, hostesses or busboys filling your water glass every five minutes. It's a place to be alone and left alone. But you can meet people at Clifton's, too. In fact, during the early years of the century, the state societies held their meetings at Clifton's and Boos Brothers cafeterias. Lonely immigrants from Iowa and Nebraska could meet other lonely immigrants from "back home." Friendships and romances were kindled over plates of macaroni and cheese and tapioca dessert cups.

Los Angeles probably didn't invent the cafeteria, but it did invent urban loneliness. Clifton's was the place that made loneliness work. It is still that kind of place.

I pushed my tray around the rails of the various steam tables looking for a meal. I settled on the chicken fried steak, mashed potatoes and canned vegetables. I got an iced tea to drink and a berry cobbler for my dessert.

I found an *LA Times* on an empty table. I sat down next to it and picked it up. I scanned the front page of the Metro section. There was a firsthand account of a Bloods gang crack house operation, a story on a forest fire in a nearby canyon that was entering its third day, and a yuppie murder-for-hire trial that had been running page one in both the news and feature sections for more than a week.

I didn't think about Coates and his conspiracy tale until I got to the cobbler. I tried to tell myself it was just another *COMET* story. Maybe a very big *COMET* story, but a *COMET* story just the same. I tried to convince myself to just write it up and move on. Don't get involved, I said. Rules number one, two and three in the newspaper game. At the *COMET* we don't second guess our sources. We just write them up. "Don't think—write!" That's one of the Barfman's many commandments. "Turds and words," he is fond of saying. "They're both just crap." And he's right. Whether it is a piece on a guy who spontaneuosly bursts into flames for the *COMET* or a Nicaraguan defector telling a staged press conference about Sandinista human rights abuses for the *Times*, the rule is the same—file it and forget it.

But Coates' story was so outrageous and he was such a frightened and pathetic man, I couldn't just move on, write my story and forget it. Maybe that's what the Barfman meant when he said "don't screw up."

I got a cup of coffee to go with my cobbler. I read the rest of the *Times*. It helped me to think about not screwing up. If anyone should know about not screwing up, it should be the people at the *Times*, right?

I finished my meal, the paper and the shoving match with my conscience. I wandered around downtown for awhile before heading back to my car. I looked at my watch. Coates' train was due to leave in a half-hour. I drove to Union Station.

75

It was always a treat to go to the train station. It is one of America's few remaining grand, high-ceilinged train stations built in the 1930s. . Terrazzo floors, dark wood benches, decorative ceilings with rich wooden beams. It was the sort of place where you could imagine bumping into William Powell and Myrna Loy.

I checked the departure board. There were only two trains leaving between 3:30 and 4:30, I hung around to nearly five. I didn't see Coates. He could have gotten by me, but I had the departure platform pretty well scoped. Maybe he was out celebrating. After all I had enriched his bank account by $2700 in the past two days. Maybe he was in a gin mill somewhere laughing up the sleeve of a new $400 suit. I didn't know and I didn't much care. I felt I had been stood up. Besides, I had a story to write.

I picked up the Hollywood Freeway from Union Station. I switched to the Harbor a few exits later and crawled along to the Santa Monica Freeway two miles south. The sound of honking horns and helicopter blades blared above the traffic report I was listening to on KNX. I don't know why they bother. It's always the same—jammed solid. The exhaust fumes from 100,000 automobiles built a monoxide curtain between me and the sinking sun. The sky was turning from dirty dish-water blue to a peach and orange swirl. It would last an hour, maybe more. It was beautiful to look at, but the price in freeway stress, all-news radio blather and carbon monoxide cocktails was too much to pay. LA was a place where you could die in your car watching the most beautiful sunsets in the hemisphere.

Thirty minutes later I crept off the freeway at La Cienega Boulevard. I took Washington the rest of the way into Venice. I was almost to the Coast Highway when I noticed I was being tailed. He was two cars back, but it looked a lot the Mercury that had tried to kill me.

I turned off the radio and stiffened in my seat. My senses came alive. "Remember, Toast, you know what I know. They will want to kill you, too." Coates' parting

76

words hung in my brain like an open gate to the part that is responsible for paranoia and panic.

I made an unexpected turn, sped up and turned again. I ended up in Ralph's parking lot. I didn't see the Mercury, but that didn't mean anything.

I went into the grocery store like nothing was happening. I bought a couple of onion rolls, a big tub of jello parfait, a half-pound of pastrami and some beer. I put the bag on my shoulder as I left the store to shield my face from the gangsters in the big Mercury. Any people in any big Mercury.

I started up my car and drove slowly to the exit of the parking lot. I couldn't see anything behind me but a Toyota full of teenagers. I smiled, adjusted my rearview mirror and pulled out into the traffic. At the first stop light I looked into the mirror again. I had just turned on the radio and was listening to the Dodgers game. I swallowed hard when the Mercury came into view. Or at least it was *a* Mercury. It was the same silvery blue color. It was right behind me. A woman sat behind the wheel. A man sat beside her. I just knew he was the type who wouldn't hesitate to shoot a gun out the window of a moving car.

All cars except French Citroens look alike to me. I can distinguish shapes, but little else. I know Mercurys because that was the family car when I was growing up. My father would never think of buying anything else.

I figured I could try to outmaneuver it again. I could drive all night or go directly to the nearest police station and dare the Mercury to do something. If it was a game of wits, I could take care of myself. But I had seen what that kind of cat-and-mouse business had done to Coates. I wasn't going to let the CIA or anyone else who might be in the Mercury turn me into a screaming paranoid.

I drove at normal speed and took the most direct route to my apartment. The Mercury followed at a safe distance. I pulled to the curb and parked right in front of my apartment. I could see its prowling headlight beams approaching from two blocks away. I got out and stood beside my car and waited for the Mercury. I couldn't see it at first, but it was the Mercury, all right. No doubt about that. A hissing cougar stalking its prey. I planted my feet in the pavement and curled my finger tips. "Come on," I muttered to myself. "If you're car enough!"

The Mercury appeared to be picking up speed as it approached me. My heart was pounding like the steel drums at a Brazilian carnival. I was scared. And well I should have been. The only thing I had for protection was a half-pound of pastrami. But I wasn't going to run.

The Mercury bore down on me. I froze in the beam of its headlights. I felt as helpless as a prairie dog on a Wyoming interstate. Helpless and ready at the same time. Me and my pastrami.

I stepped from the side of my car into the street and into the path of the on-rushing Mercury. It blasted its horn and swerved to miss me. As it sped off I heard a voice trailing from the passenger side of the car. "Asshole!"

Chapter 12

I couldn't concentrate on my dinner or the Dodgers game. LA fell behind early and stayed there. The Dodgers are a good lot and I like Vin Scully who broadcasts the games, but Lasorda gives me a pain. I turned off the radio and turned on the television. Nothing but reruns of *Family Ties* and the *Cosby Show* and some network rubbish. I tried to read a book, but couldn't find anything interesting. I went outside and smoked a cigarette. It was nine o'clock and it was still hot. It was early in the year, but I felt a Santa Ana coming up. The Santa Anas are hot winds that blow through the Southland and make people hot and irritable, even a little crazy.

There are a number of hot, dry winds around the world that are said to drive people temporarily loco. There is one in Switzerland. And the Mistral is a hot wind that blows up the Rhone River in the South of France.

I read an article once that talked about what those winds do to people. But you have to consider the locations. Switzerland is as normal as a right turn on a red light. So is the South of France. But Los Angeles is full of the deranged, the criminal and the borderline psychotic to begin with. When the Santa Anas blow all hell can break loose. Stranglers, slashers, former Mansonites prowl the streets when the winds blow. And even the normal can get jumpy. Raymond Chandler put his finger on it when he wrote "The Santa Anas make your nerves jump and your skin itch and meek little housewives run their fingers over the edge of carving knives and study the back of their husbands' necks." Anything can happen in LA and when the Santa Anas blow, it usually does.

The heat made me irritable and restless. The sounds of the neighborhood annoyed me. I went back into my apartment for a beer. I called Marty Angelo to find out if he learned anything about the Mercury. There was no answer at his place. I went through my pockets looking for a book of matches for a second cigarette. I pulled out a small envelope. On one side was the telephone number of Coates' aunt. I turned it over. The envelope was addressed to Coates. His address was typed in plain letters. There was only one thing to do.

Coates lived in Echo Park just north of downtown. In a general way, it was between Dodger Stadium, which wasn't actually in Echo Park, and Aimee Semple McPherson's Angeles Temple of the Four Square Church, which was. Baseball and flim-flam religion with lots of corn. I always liked the idea of Echo Park for those reasons.

Coates' house was on a noisy little street just off the Hollywood Freeway. The neighborhood might have been up-to-date when Aimee was packing them in at the Temple, but that was sixty years ago. The neighborhood had been on a slow, downhill slide for years.

I walked up the steps to the small stucco bungalow and knocked on the door. Some inside lights were on. I tried to think of something to say while I waited. I wanted to know why he hadn't taken the afternoon train. I wanted to know if he was running a con on me and the *COMET*. I wanted to hear the rest of his story. I wanted him to convince me he wasn't a banana fritter.

I knocked a second time, but still no one came to the door. I called out my name in case he were cowering inside the door. I knocked again. This knock was loud enough to have created a public disturbance. Maybe he had taken the train after all. Just as a parting gesture, I gave the door handle a twist. It turned and the door opened. I pushed it. It gave a friendly, noisy squeak as I opened it halfway. I stepped inside and called out Coates' name.

I continued cautiously into the small house until I was mugged by the powerful smell of burnt coffee. The room was furnished by the Salvation Army. A thrift store couch, a thrift store recliner, a thrift store rug and some thrift store end tables. It was all very cheesy, except for the sound system. I don't know anything about stereos and speakers, but I do recognize expensive. Expensive, like Japanese with dozens of silver buttons, switches and digital displays. Next to the turntable/ amplifier/tape deck combination was a large case of record albums. I pulled some out at random-- *Clambake, Elvis' Christmas Album, Are You Lonesome Tonight?* Every one of the records, and there must have been two hundred of them, were Elvis Presley recordings. Single 45s, LP albums, greatest hits, his movie soundtracks, everything Elvis had ever recorded seemed to be in Coates' front room.

I left the living room and walked down the short hall. I stopped at the first room. The door had a large, broken padlock swinging from a bracket above the doorknob.

I opened the door and flipped on the light switch. I stepped into what can only be described as a museum. An Elvis Presley museum. The walls had been made over into a giant four-corner mural of Elvis' record album covers and movie posters. Some were mounted in frames while others were laminated and hung flush with the wall.

The contents of the room was a curated collection of Elvis dolls, wigs, table lamps, ashtrays, a blue neon sign that flickered "Love Me Tender," and a dozen *COMET*-sized scrap books bursting with yellowing newspaper and magazine clippings piled on a table in the center of the room. A fifty-volume library of books on Elvis and rock and roll stood against the far wall in

81

a small oak book case. An actual-size guitar with Elvis' picture hand-painted on it hung from the ceiling like a chandelier.

Graceland in Echo Park? It looked like the only thing missing was Elvis Presley's casket. I retreated into the hallway. I peeked into the kitchen. The smell of sour and burnt coffee nearly put me under. A box of donuts was sitting on the table. The sink was piled high with dirty dishes. I went to the stove. I could see a very low flame under a quart saucepan. I turned it off. A slick brown ring of coffee had fused to the bottom of the pan. A little voice told me I should leave Coates' place. A larger voice told me there was still more of the house to explore.

I walked down the hallway toward the back of the house. One room was a small bathroom. The other was a bedroom. The door was open, but it was dark and I couldn't see in. The smell of dirty clothes stood guard at the threshold of the room. I could hear cars whizzing past on the nearby freeway. I extended an arm into the room. It groped along the wall looking for the light switch. When it found it, it flipped it on.

A dingy yellow, under-watted overhead bulb reclaimed the room from the darkness. The place looked like a victim of an earthquake. Clothes were strewn over every inch of the floor. A cheap cardboard wardrobe closet lay on its side. A chair was overturned and the mattress on the bed hung over the box springs at an unnatural angle.

Lying on top of the bed, on top of the rumpled and soiled covers was Coates. He was on his back. He was stiff and his open eyes were fixed on the ceiling. His right arm hung awkwardly off the bed. I walked over to him and felt for a pulse. It wasn't really necessary. He was cold to the touch. I shivered in the musty heat of his room. I sat down on the edge of the bed to think. Also to calm myself and reorganize. Next to the bed was a small nightstand. There were two small bottles on it. Pill bottles. Empty pill bottles. I picked them up and read the labels. One was Dilauddid and the other was a barbituate with an unpronounceable name. I had heard their names before.

It didn't make sense. A guy who was constantly wired up was an unlikely candidate to take an overdose of sleeping pills. It especially didn't make sense for a man who was in a panicked hurry to leave town. A man who had reservations on the afternoon train. A person like that—like Coates—doesn't take an overdose of sleeping pills.

I remembered where I had heard about Dilauddid. It was one of the drugs that Elvis overdosed on. I read about it in the *COMET* library and Sherm had mentioned it. Was this some sort of copycat suicide? It might have made some bizarre sense if Coates believed Elvis Presley died of an overdose.

I remembered something else. Something I didn't want to remember. Something Coates said about the CIA. "They will make you dead. In a car accident on the freeway, a fall down the stairs, an overdose of prescription pills." A coincidence, or did the man really know what he was talking about?

I could feel the sweat beading up on my neck at the shirt collar. In the distance I heard sirens. They were coming closer. I left the bedroom and walked briskly through the house to the front door. I exited very nonchalantly down the front steps and walked to my car. I pulled out into the traffic just as two police squad cars turned into Coates' driveway. If I thought there was even a remote chance the cops would have believed my story—Coates' story—I would have stayed and talked to them. Fat chance! I hit the Hollywood Freeway and rode it all the way out to Van Nuys before I had built up enough nerve to exit and back track toward Venice.

Chapter 13

I didn't go home. I couldn't. I needed to think, but I couldn't do that either. At least, not rationally. I just wanted to drive and smoke cigarettes, but that got boring after an hour.

I tried not to think of Coates' death in terms of what he had told me. What he had predicted would happen. However, seeing his body stretched out on his bed made thinking about anything else impossible. His death gave a certain credulity to his wild tale about the CIA and Elvis Presley that he could not provide when he was alive.

I headed for the RIO office. The Research Investigation Organization was located between downtown and Culver City, just off Crenshaw. It researched political assassinations and conspiracies. Its many critics said it invented them, but RIO was responsible for re-opening the assassination of Robert Kennedy a few years ago and was among the first groups to fill in the blanks on Oliver North and the Iran-Contra business. A few state legislators and U.S. Congressmen relied on information supplied by RIO. Its detractors said they were kooks and referred to it as "Conspiracies R Us."

Basically, RIO was a two-man operation. I knew one of them—Gilbert Talavera. I met him five years ago when I had that brief stint with the *Times*. He and Danny Jones, the other half of RIO, were trying to reopen the investigation in the fiery deaths of the five Symbionese Liberation Army members. They were barbecued by the LAPD in a house in Watts. RIO claimed there was substantial information to indicate the California CID, the state's version of the FBI, had actually created the strange little band of urban guerrillas who had murdered the superintendent of the Oakland school system and kidnapped Patty Hearst.

The *Times* gave the story big play when a former CID man came in from the cold and substantiated many of RIO's claims. A couple of state assemblymen got behind RIO's demand to begin a citizens' investigation.

I spent a week on the story and watched it blow away like the head of a spent dandelion when the CID man was discredited as a mental case. I stayed in touch with Gilbert over the years. Actually, he stayed in touch with me. He would phone every few months with some new or updated conspiracy theory he wanted to publicize. It didn't matter to Gilbert that I was working at the *COMET* and not the *Times*, he was looking for any media outlets that would give RIO cases some coverage.

It was getting late, but I knew Gilbert worked at the RIO office well into the night. The office was behind a bakery. It was open to the public, but the public didn't know where it was. I did.

I walked in the front door. Gilbert was hunched over a computer terminal clacking information into it. Reams of printout paper were coiled on the floor like like giant planed wood shavings. Cigarette butts in ashtrays, empty paper caoffee cups and loose files were spread over the office's two desks and bookcases like lawn fertilizer. The walls were bare except for a large black and white poster of Martin Luther King lying dead on the balcony of that Memphis motel with some of his lieutenants huddled around the body while others stood pointing extended arms in the direction of the assassin's shot.

"Be with you in a minute," Gilbert said, his back to me. "Take a seat if you can find one."

"Joe Brody sent me," I said, using the name of the character played by Warren Beatty in *The Parallax View*, the ultimate conspiracy film. It was Gilbert Talavera's favorite film. He stopped what he was doing and spun around in his chair.

"Steve Toast!" he exclaimed. He smiled and got to his feet to shake hands. "Long time no see, dude. How you been keeping? I thought maybe the Accuracy in Media goons had canceled your subscription."

"Nah, they're only interested in newspapers held hostage by Moscow gold. Like the New York *Times*."

"I heard that. What's been happenin', man? I was going to give you a call next week. I'm working on a hot new lead in the Agca case."

"The guy who shot the Pope?"

"Yeah. We've linked him to people who work at the Institute for Strategic Studies at Georgetown University. You know, these are the dudes who pop up on McNeil-Lehrer and Koppel as experts on international terrorism."

"What about the Bulgarians?"

"Pure frijoles, man. It's the old Catholic Church-CIA story. They were real tight for thirty years, you know. Then along comes this Polish *pachuco* and says 'nyet', or whatever the Polish word for 'no' is. The CIA felt betrayed and cut off from one of its primary intelligence sources. It all makes sense for the CIA to hit the Pope and then use their academic whores at Georgetown to cover their tracks and point the finger at the Bulgarians, and by implication, the Russians. Do you know who Agca met in West Germany just one month before the attempted assassination?"

"Whoa, there, Gilbert," I said, holding up my hands and signaling for a time out. "This is all very fascinating, but I didn't come by for pope dope. When you get it done, boil it down to two pages and send it to me. Maybe we can use it. Might have to tie it with something else, like the Shroud of Turin hoax."

"You got it, Cisco." Talavera went over to one of the desks and rooted around the effluvia for a cigarette. He found a crumpled pack under some files. He shook one out and lit it before sitting down in the closest chair. He pointed to a folding chair that was leaning up against the wall. I walked over and picked it up and returned to Gilbert's desk.

"That one's got a bent hinge or something," he said. "Watch how you sit in it."

I watched how I unfolded it and how I sat in it. "Gilbert, what do you know about a CIA plot to snuff Jimmy Carter?"

Gilbert leaned back in his chair. He took a long drag from his cigarette and blew the smoke out of the side of his mouth. "There were a couple," he said. "Which one do you want to know about?"

"You mean there really was a plot?"

"Hey, man, you brought it up."

"And there was more than one?"

"Since none of them got very far, it is not high priority research. What the Company did was kill his political career. They were behind the hostage deal in Iran."

"Get out! The CIA arranged for the kidnapping of Americans?"

"No, not the taking of the hostages, but sabotaging every effort to free them. Bush made a secret trip to Paris in the fall of 1980, just before the election. He met the Ayatollah's people and promised them $40 million in cash and $5 billion in arms sales if Iran would not release the hostages until after the election. Man, it was in the newspapers not all that long ago. It was the failure to release the hostages that elected Reagan and sent Carter back to Georgia."

"What about Elvis Presley?"

"What about him?"

"Does he figure into any of this? Any of the CIA plots against Carter?"

"You serious, man, or you just jerking my chain?"

"I'm serious. A man I met told me Elvis Presley knew about a CIA plot to kill Carter and the Agency killed him to shut him up."

"Who? Elvis? Guitar, long sideburns? We talking about the same guy?"

"Yeah."

"Okay, I'll bite. How did Elvis Presley find out about a CIA plan to kill the President? That's not information you're likely to pick up at a recording studio."

"James Earl Ray told him."

Gilbert Talavera looked at me like a lot of people must have looked at him when he told them about the Kennedy assassinations or conspiracies led by World War II nazi war criminals hiding out in Bolivia. I spent the next fifteen minutes telling him everything Coates had told me. By the time I had finished Gilbert looked like he was experiencing a narcotic high.

Without a word he got up from his chair and walked to the metal filing cabinets on the other side of the room. He pulled three or four folders and took them to the computer terminal. For five minutes he entered data taken from the folders. I felt like I should have said something, but I didn't want to break his concentration.

"Toast," he said, finally. "Come here." I walked over to where he was sitting. "I think you might be on to something, Steve," he said into the display monitor screen. "Look at this."

"What?" I said, looking at the screen.

"I plugged the info I have on Ray into the three Carter assassination scenarios that I know about. He accesses quite nicely with the first one, the one your man told you about. Especially his connection with Johnny Crackers. See, I entered his file and he checks out. He was in prison with Ray and he is on our list as a shooter for the Company. And interestingly, enough, he was killed in a prison stabbing on August 18, 1977."

"Two days after Elvis died."

"Right!"

"Some of the other stuff your man told you checks out, too. Look at this." Gilbert scrolled down the screen. "The link between Buckley Bergeron and the Cubans. They were in New York in January 1977. I don't know if they had dinner at Toots Shor's, but I did a random check on the death of Herbert Matthews and Freddie Prinze."

"And?"

"And their deaths sound fishy to me. That's all I can say at this point. I don't have enough data."

"Does this mean the CIA could have killed Elvis Presley?"

Gilbert turned off the screen and turned around. "I start with that assumption, man. Realistically, at this point, all we say for sure is that there was a CIA plot to ice Carter. It is quite possible that James Earl Ray learned about it from Johnny Crackers. It is also possible that Ray contacted Elvis and told him. And if the Company knew that Elvis was hip to them and that he was going to go public, it doesn't take a leap of faith to believe that they got to him."

"You mean killed him?"

"It is a possibility, but, like I said, I just don't have enough data. Give me a few days on this. I have a contact in Chicago who researches the deaths of famous people. I'm sure he's got something on Elvis Presley."

"I'd be grateful, Gilbert. Anything you can get, as soon as you can get it."

"I dig. Give me a day or two. I like this. It is a scenario that has wings. I think you might be on to something big, Toast."

"As big as the Kennedy assassination?"

"If it checks out, bigger. Much bigger. Kennedy was only a President, not the King of Rock and Roll."

Gilbert Talavera had that narcotic high look again. It was the look of a man who had one foot in conspiracy theory heaven. It was at that point I told him the potential price of heaven.

"The man who told me this is dead," I said, bluntly.

"Dead? How?"

"It looked like a drug overdose, but he told me the CIA was going to hit him and make it look like an accident. It could have been just that, an accident, but I have a creepy feeling it wasn't. What do you think?"

"I know that if Buckley Bergeron had anything to do with it, it was no accident. This man has planted more bodies in boot hill than Billy the Kid. He's the guy the Israelis used to turn to when they wanted someone dead in a hurry and couldn't afford to do it themselves."

"Do you really think he might be involved?"

"Who knows? No one in the intelligence research community has heard anything about him since the early 1980s. He just disappeared."

"Do you know any agents named Javert?"

"No, but I will run a check." He took out a pencil and wrote the name on a scrap of paper.

"You know, I've been followed at least once since I met this guy Coates."

"I don't run license plates."

"No. A big silver blue Mercury, I think it took a shot at me. It was either the Mercury or the other one."

"What the hell are you talking about?"

"I don't know. I'm just telling you this so you will be careful. There are a lot of strange things happening."

Gilbert snorted through his nose. "Look, chico, I've been following nazi war criminals, corporate killers, CIA and KGB plots for twenty years. Ever since the cops blew away brother Salazar during the Chicano Moratorium in '70 and tried to cover it up. Man, we know they're after us. The paranoids only think people are after them. We've got proof. We're careful, but how do you protect against fire-bombs?"

"Yeah, I heard you were fire-bombed."

"Twice in the last year. They didn't do all that much damage, but, hey, it still scares the shit out of you. But you've got to keep on keeping on, as they say."

Gilbert tried to tell me more about his new findings concerning the 1981 assassination attempt on John Paul II, but I wasn't in the mood. I told him again I would do my best to run it in the *COMET*.

The smell of fresh bread from the bakery filled my nose. The bakers on the night shift were hard at work. The aroma took me back to a dozen great meals where I

had hot, buttered, right-out-of-the-oven bread or biscuits in my hand. A dozen great Thanksgiving meals
with my family. It temporarily chased away the stink of
fear and conspiracy and murder.

Chapter 14

I took the Santa Monica Freeway into downtown LA and headed straight for the Times-Mirror Building, home of the Los Angeles *Times*. The *LA Times*, the west coast pillar of responsible American journalism. The best newspaper in the west. The newspaper that invented boomtown and boostertown Los Angeles. And Harrison Gray Otis was the man who invented the *Times*. Otis and Harry Chandler, his son-in-law.

Otis was a narrow-minded, bile-spewing, labor-loathing crusader for neanderthal causes and fellow in good standing of the great nineteenth century newspaper editor-publishers who manufactured public opinion and battered the masses into consensus. The Otis, the Pulitzer and the Hearst consensus. Yellow journalism, jingoism and lurid headlines. That was the way they did things and Otis was among the best. He and his cronies were the spiritual grandparents of the tabloids as well as the great American dailies we have come to honor and respect. Otis was a primary donor to that genetic journalistic sperm bank that produced the *National COMET.*

However, three generations of Otis-Chandlers since the old man died have slowly and methodically taken the *Times* from the Dark Ages into the Age of Enlightenment. It is a reasonable, responsible and respectable newspaper. But it couldn't be that respectable. It hired me. I worked for the *Times* when I first came to Los Angeles. In fact, that's why I came to LA. But it wasn't a real job, so when they let me go, it wasn't a real firing. I was hired to fill-in for a journalist who had broken his back in an auto accident. When he recovered and was ready to return to work, it was 'Adios, Toast.' One day I was writing a story about smog, the next day I was living in the street eating it. But that's the way it goes in the newspaper world. The *Times* never promised me a rose garden, but I didn't expect to land on the sidewalk chin first, either.

Anyway, I still know a few people at the *Times*. Especially the guys on graveyard, the shift I worked for most of the time. I even know the security guards. Rick Dickstein was still working the city desk. I called him from the lobby and he beamed me up to the city room.

I spent a few minutes with him and two other guys I knew. They enjoyed cracking jokes about the *COMET*. Dickstein said my story about the exploding priest was Pulitzer material, but he didn't really mean it. They all had a good laugh. I just thought about Harrison Gray Otis and that day in 1942 when the *Times* reported that LA was under attack from Japanese warplanes. It went to far as to "report" an enemy airplane had been shot down near 185th and Vermont Avenue.

It took some talking, but I got Dickstein to let me into the *Times* library. I didn't tell him what I wanted. I just let him squeeze off a few more jokes about the *COMET*. I laughed harder than anybody. It made them all feel good.

I found my way around the library without much trouble. Nothing much had changed and what had was fairly simple to figure out. I started working the file drawers. I pulled everything I could find on the CIA during the first year of the Carter presidency. I also retrieved files on Angola, Panama, Cuba, David Berkowitz, James Earl Ray, Freddie Prinze and Elvis Presley's death.

Dickstein came in about two hours later to check up on me. He wanted to make it clear that he had absolutely no curiosity about what I was doing. However, he made a point to express his concern about what I was doing to the *Times* library. He observed that I had enough files out and microfilm readers in operation to hire an extra staff librarian to refile everything. He pleaded with me to be sure to put everything back in its proper place. His eyes wandered over the clipping files I had opened. He said something about a Pulitzer Prize again and went back to the city room.

I poured over hundreds of newspaper articles and reels of microfilm. I lost track of time. I checked everything I could remember from Coates' story. I worked methodically and haphazardly at the same time. I checked names, dates, relationships both in chronological order and randomly as they popped into my head. I went over CIA stories looking for a pattern and articles about Carter's foreign policy looking for a provocation. I tracked James Earl Ray for the three days of his escape from prison and studied the controversy and confusion surrounding Elvis' death and botched autopsy.

By four in the morning my eyes had gone into a stare mode and my brain had short-circuited from memory overload. I caught myself dozing off in the middle of articles I was reading for the third time.

I gathered up the files and replaced the ones I could remember taking. The others I placed in the refile basket. The microfilm spools lay sprawled over the tables next to the reading machines. I put some of them back in the microfilm drawer before fatigue tapped me on the shoulder and told me to forget it. I tidied up the place as best I could before leaving. Shelly Bubblefarb would have killed me if I had done this to the *COMET* library. Dickstein wouldn't have been too happy, either, but I exited down the back stairs. I didn't want to talk to him or the others. I didn't want to explain what I had been doing in the *Times* library for all those hours. I don't think I could have explained what I was doing even if I had really wanted to. And I couldn't tell them what I had found. I wasn't sure of that myself.

94

Chapter 15

It wasn't light yet when I pulled into the Venice Archipelago, but night was breaking up. I made a straight line for my bedroom, stopping only momentarily to open the front door of my apartment. My plan was to sleep until someone from the *COMET* called and threatened to fire me if I didn't come in to work. I vaguely remembered that I was supposed to be in early, but I couldn't remember why. I drew the curtains and tore off my clothes. I was unconscious the moment I pulled up the covers.

I had fitful dreams about nuclear war and was being chased for a murder I actually did commit. It was all that running. It tired me out and plunged me into a deeper sleep. I don't know how long the phone had been ringing when I sent out an arm on an expeditionary mission to find it.

"Hello," I said, putting something in my ear. I prayed it was the phone receiver.

"Hi, Steve. I'm glad I caught you at home." It was a cheery female voice. A sweet voice, a friendly voice. I had no idea who it was.

"I'm on my way in," I said. At least that's what I thought I said. It's what I wanted to say, but I was still semi-conscious. My mouth felt like a cafe full of French intellectuals chain-smoking Gauloise cigarettes.

"Steve," the voice continued. "It's been a long time. Much too long. I hope I haven't called at a bad time." I still had no idea who it was. Maybe it was the new receptionist in the executive office and she was being sarcastic with me.

"Tell the Barfman I'll be there in an hour. I was working late. Cut me some slack, okay?" I nearly fell back asleep.

"Steve. What are you talking about? It's me, Jan."

Jan? The new receptionist was named Billie or Bunny or something. Jan? The only Jan I could remember was an ex-girlfriend named Jan. My mother's name is Janice, but we've always been "Mom" and "Stevie" to each other.

"Jan who?" I said, to protect myself. I was starting to come out of it. My eyes were open and I knew where I was.

"Jan who?" the voice giggled. "It hasn't been that long, Steve. Do you have someone there with you? I can call later if this is a bad time."

"No, no." I sat up in the bed. It was Jan. My Jan. Or rather, my ex-Jan. Jan Thomas. I hadn't spoken to her in almost three years. "I thought you were in D.C.?"

"Did I wake you up? I'm sorry."

"Me? No. Just laying here in the old bed reading some Alice Walker. I don't handle broken concentration very well. What time is it anyway?"

"It's a little before nine."

"A.m. or p.m.?"

"Are you all right, Steve? You sound so strange."

"How would you know how I sound? We haven't spoken to each other in three years."

"Just over two, actually," she interrupted.

My voice began to rise. "Then you call me in the middle of the night and tell me I sound strange."

"I'm sorry, Steve. Maybe it was a bad idea to call. I can see you still have some things to work out. Did you ever go to Dr. Blesser, like I suggested?"

"Dr. who?"

"You remember. The Anger Therapy Institute in Santa Monica."

"For chrissakes!"

96

"I think he might be able to help you."

"I don't need help, Jan. I need sleep."

"Right. I'm sorry for intruding into your life. I have no right."

"Forget it. What are you doing back in town? Last time I heard you landed a big job with the *Washington Post*"

"I did. They've sent me back to head up the Southern California Bureau."

"They did? When was that?"

"Oh, uh, I've been back for awhile."

"How long?"

"Oh, I don't know. Oh, okay, about a year, if you must know."

"That long?"

"I wanted to call. I really did. I must have picked up the phone a hundred times."

"Spare me, Jan. You don't owe me anything. Oh, except maybe the Trivial Pursuit game. You did take it with you when you split, didn't you?"

"It was mine."

"Like hell it was. I bought it at Games N' Stuff in Hollywood."

"Steve! My mother sent it to me for Christmas the year we lived in Westwood. Remember we stayed up till 3 am...."

"I still have the goddamn receipt!" I was one decibel below a shout. "Do you want me to show it to you?"

"Steve, calm down. This is ridiculous. I didn't call to get into an argument over the ownership of a silly old game."

"You didn't? What did you call to argue about?"

Jan laughed. "I see you still have your sense of humor."

"It's the only thing you left behind when you moved out."

"Steve! Please! I called as a friend. Can't we be friends?"

"Sure. You want to go to a ball game or something?" I'm not sure I intended to be so sarcastic. It just

97

came out that way. She gave me such a good setup, it was hard to turn it down.

But it had been years since I last saw her. The six months before that, the relationship had degenerated into a long brawl, interrupted only occasionally by periods of sleep. I forget all the things we argued about. Politics, money, movies, you name it. But the big thing was career. The "C" word. We were both at the *Times*. Jan was on her way to the top, while I was on my way to the pavement. She was a bright, aggressive young journalist on the move. I was on the move, too, only my move was to the *COMET*.

Maybe I resented her success. I know she resented my "failure." Maybe I hated her eagerness to suck up to anyone who was in a position to advance her career. Maybe I couldn't stand her holier-than-me attitude. Whatever it was, we split and she took my Trivial Pursuit among many other things.

"Steve," she said. "I just called to say 'hi' and to ask you if you wanted to get together for a friendly drink sometime."

"Jan, what is this all about? Is something up?"

"Well, to be perfectly honest, I stopped by the *Times* this morning and bumped into Rick Dickstein and he—"

"He told you I was snooping around the *Times* library in the small hours of the morning acting like a mad man."

"No. He just said you stopped by. It was just the push I needed to pick up the telephone for the 101st time."

"Just like that, eh?"

"What else? Steve, you were always so suspicious. Just because we split up doesn't mean I hate you and don't care about you."

"Really? I thought that's what breaking up was all about."

"Honestly, Steve. Lighten up. How about that drink?"

"Yeah, why not? For old time's sake, right?"

"Exactly. I'd really like to hear what you've been doing since the last time we saw each other."

"Didn't Dickstein tell you I am still at the *COMET*?"

"Well, yes."

"And you still want to talk to me? I'm flattered."

"I've mellowed a lot since we split up. Really. I've come down from Mount Olympus and joined the real world."

"Saw the trashy things they do at the *Post*, eh?"

"Not exactly. I'm just not as judgmental as I once was."

"Do you know Woodward?"

"Bob hasn't worked for the *Post* since the mid '80s."

"Bob, is it?"

"How about this afternoon?"

"What about it?"

"Our drink."

"Oh, yeah. Sure. Fine."

"Want to do lunch while we're at it? It's all on me. What do you say?"

"Whatever you say."

"Super. It's settled then. Do you know where Garbo's is?"

"Not exactly."

"Everybody goes there."

"I guess that's why I don't know where it is."

"It's in Century City."

"It's all coming back."

"Why don't I meet you there. Say one-ish?"

"Okay. Why not. One-ish."

"Great. Ciao for now, Steve."

"Yeah. Ciao for now."

I hung up the phone. I called the *COMET* and told the Barfman's secretary I was working on the Elvis story at home and wouldn't be in until later. Like much later. I hoped he would buy it, but I didn't really care. The taste of an old romance hung sourly in my mouth. I went to the bathroom to take a pee and brush my teeth. Then I went back to bed until eleven-thirty.

Chapter 16

I was getting up anyway when I heard the knocking at the door. It was a persistent and insinuating knock like the knock of the Jehovah's Witnesses. Mom used to herd us kids into the deepest corner of the back bedroom when she heard that knock. But sometimes, even hiding in the bedroom didn't work. Even when we held our breath. Sooner or later, like death and taxes, the knock of the Jehovahs would get us.

I didn't care. I was an adult. I answered knocks at my door. Most of the time, anyway. I got out of bed and put on the jogging suit Jan gave me for Christmas the year she was a running nut. I looked through the peep-hole in the front door. I saw two men wearing suits. They looked like commodity brokers. Something else I didn't need.

I opened the door. The taller and older man standing at the center of the outside step smiled broadly.

"Good morning, sir," he said. "My name is Reverend Thurley Swale. And this is Twin Brother Osgood." He motioned to the young blond man at his side who didn't look anything like him.

"Sorry, Reverend," I said, shaking my head. "I'm a raving atheist. Madalyn Murray O'Hair is my mother-in-law." I began to close the door. Even the Jehovahs get discouraged with that line. Reverend Swale opened the screen door and put his right foot forward. He must have graduated from the Vacuum Cleaner Salesmen School of Religious Recruiting. "If we could just have one small minute of your time, brother."

"Sorry," I said. "My wife's on a heart-lung machine and it just broke. I've got to take her to the hospital."

Swale wouldn't take 'get lost' for an answer. "Just one small minute. We'd like to tell you about the good news of our ministry. We are from the Jesus is in Galilee Church."

"Get your foot out of my door, reverend, or you'll be getting it back in the mail."

Swale slowly backed up. There was a pleading look in his eyes. "Jesus Christ rose on the third day," he said, as he reached into his pocket. I rolled my eyes. Okay, he was going to give me some mindless Bible tract and leave. It was a deal I could live with.

However, there was no Bible tract in his pocket. It looked more like a .32, as in handgun. "I think you should invite us to step inside, brother. We want to share our good news with you."

"Tell you what," I said, throwing open the door. "Why don't you two guys from God come on inside. I'll make us some ice tea and we can swap psalms."

Swale smiled and stepped inside. "Thank you, that is very kind. The tea, however, won't be necessary."

"Whatever you say. Have your friend come in, too. Twin Brother Osgood, wasn't it? Anything for you?" The younger man shook his head. I directed them to chairs in the living room. I sat on the sofa. There was a moment of silence. Just the four of us—Swale, his twin brother, me and the gun. "So," I said. "What's the good news?"

Swale smiled. It was the smile televangelists wear. It's called the 'Pat Robertson Grin.' A grin and a gun. That was a winning combination to advance anyone's ministry. However, I had the feeling that this wasn't the latest high pressure tactic to increase financial pledges.

"The Lord works in mysterious ways," Swale said, "his wonders to perform."

"Amen," said Twin Brother Osgood, showing the first signs of life.

"Do you know the work of the Jesus is in Galilee Church, brother?"

"Tell you the truth, reverend, I've been out of touch with that kind of stuff. If you will leave me some literature I promise to read it and get back to you. In the meantime, would you accept money? Do you think twenty is enough to get you to put away that gun?"

Swale just smiled. "Sit down, Brother Toast. We don't want your money. We just want to talk."

My body stiffened. I don't mind the bank and the phone company knowing my name. Or even those boiler room telemarketers who call up and try to sell me rumba lessons and lifetime supplies of carpet shampoo. Well, actually, I do mind, but it is something I can live with. It comes with having your telephone number listed. But crazed Bible-thumpers with guns! That was too much. Sweat broke into little beads on my forehead. My throat was as dry as the LA River in August and I felt a little dizzy.

"How do you know my name?" I asked. Swale smiled and said nothing. "More of the Lord's mysterious ways?"

"Mr. Toast, we are men of the Lord. Men of peace and brotherhood. We come to share His ways with you and ask your assistance in a matter of pressing concern."

"Help? I told you I was an atheist. Well, actually, maybe not quite an atheist. I have a lot of questions that...."

"Mr. Toast, you know something about our Lord Jesus Christ, do you not?"

"Sure. The founder of Christmas and Easter."

"Please, Mr. Toast, your sarcasm is wasted on Twin Brother Osgood and myself."

I looked at Twin Brother Osgood. He still didn't look anything like Swale. I wanted to say something, but I kept my mouth shut.

Swale continued. "Jesus is in Galilee is a small, but

expanding church, Mr. Toast. And it has expanded against enormous odds. You see, we reject Pauline Christianity as a great blasphemy that distorted the life and death of Jesus Christ for its own opportunist ends. Paul, the so-called founder of Christianity was nothing more than a collaborationist Jewish agent from Tarsus, an apostate from the law, a murderer, a defamer and persecutor of the Lord. Do you follow me?"

I shrugged my shoulders. Even if I had known what he was talking about, I wasn't going to say so.

"In the vernacular, Mr. Toast, we are a heresy to the usurpers who control the Christian church, both Catholic and Protestant. A heresy that is two thousand years old. A heresy that was brutally suppressed time and time again during the first four centuries of the so-called Christian era. But we are a heresy that knows the truth and is not afraid to speak it. We are the survivors of the early Church of James and Judas Thomas, brothers to the Lord. That is why the prevaricators and blasphemers who claim Jesus Christ as their own private property have always hated and persecuted us."

"It's a rotten world," I said, trying to cough up some sympathy. "But what has this got to do with me? We atheists believe in live and let live. I haven't persecuted anybody."

"They stole the Lord Jesus Christ and twisted and distorted everything. From denying the existence of his twin brother to the circumstances of his so-called death on the cross. It's Satan's work. Paul's work. He spread the lies throughout the Greek and Roman worlds. From his own lips in Second Corinthians, chapter 11, verses 3 and 4, he states that the emissaries of James are preaching 'another Jesus'. Indeed! There was another Jesus from the one he cynically invented and merchandised throughout the lands of the Mediterranean."

"Did you say twin brother?"

"Thomas called Didymous. Judas Thomas, twin brother of Jesus, apostle most high and fellow initiate into the hidden word of Christ. He was the second, the dual messiah."

"That's a new one on me. I saw the photos of the nativity when I was a kid. Correct me if I am wrong, but there was only one babe in the manger."

Twin Brother Osgood's nostrils flared. I thought he was going to get up from his chair and smite me. He could have, too. He looked like he might have spent some time in the UCLA backfield.

Swale continued. "We are not here to debate theology, Mr. Toast. I am attempting to tell you who we are so that we may enlist your assistance on...."

"Yes, a matter of pressing concern, right?"

"Exactly. Allow me to shock you further and tell you that Jesus Christ did not die on the cross."

I'll admit I was shocked. "Are you guys a cult or something?" I asked.

Swale ignored my comment. "Even the Paulists' own gospels tell us that if you read them properly."

"Did Sherm Bolivia put you guys up to this?"

Twin Brother Osgood stood up and rolled his shoulders. "Twin Brother Thurley," he said while looking at me. "I can't abide this blasphemer's smart mouth. May I have permission to shut it for him?"

Swale dismissed him. "Patience, Twin Brother Osgood. Sarcasm and ridicule are but the gentlest forms of persecution. I will tell you when Mr. Toast needs his mouth shut." Twin Brother Osgood rolled his shoulders again and pulled on the cuffs of his white shirt and sat down.

Swale leaned forward in his chair and looked directly into my face. "Jesus planned his own crucifixion so as to fulfill the prophecies of the Old Testament. This was necessary for him to be proclaimed the true messiah. He had no intention of dying. He spent less than three hours on the cross. His legs were not broken. He could not have died in that short a period of time. Without breaking the legs, a man could survive two to three days on the cross."

"Breaking the legs?"

"The feet of a crucified man stood on a small platform nailed to the cross. They absorbed the weight of the body. When the legs were broken, as they were with all the crucified, the weight was shifted to the lungs and the victim died of suffocation."

"Ah."

"Jesus' legs were not broken. He was taken from the cross immediately by Joseph of Arimathea, Jesus' secret disciple, and spirited away to a tomb in Joseph's own garden. When the frightened disciples had the nerve to come to the tomb, the 'body' was, of course, gone. Gone because there was no corpse. Jesus was on his way to Galilee. Did he not say to Simon Peter and the Beloved Disciple in the garden at Gethsemane, 'After I have been raised up I will go ahead of you to Galilee'. Mark, chapter 14, verse 28.

"The Savior's ministry was a conscientious plan to fulfill the prophecies of the Old Testament. That was the way— the only way— He could become the messiah. He had to be tested on the cross. Many of the Psalms foretell the crucifixion of Jesus and his survival on the cross, but the Paulists deny this simple truth.

"Jesus was both spiritual messiah and temporal King of Israel. His crucifixion sought to combine the two in the Last Times, which were a time of great social unrest for the people of Israel.

Jesus' people were in revolt against the satanic tyranny of Rome and its collaborationist Jewish leaders, called Sadduces. It is this part that Paul and the fathers of the Christian church suppressed. They turned Jesus into an icon, a legend, a cartoon character who was half-man, half-god. They couldn't even get their story straight. He is the lamb of peace in the book of Luke and in Matthew, Jesus comes 'not to bring peace, but a sword.' Luke tells us Jesus was a poor carpenter. Matthew says He was a royal descendant of David. The contradictions and fairy tale aspect of the gospels is revolting. The Jesus Christ we know today was a Hollywood creation of First Century Fox!"

I had to go to the bathroom in the worst sort of way, but I didn't want to interrupt. I have to admit Swale's story was much better than most I have heard

105

in my line of work. However, I was waiting for the other shoe to drop. The shoe that would fit my foot. Finally, Reverend Swale began to bring me into the picture.

"The Jesus is in Galilee Church," he said, "holds these and other truths about our Lord to be the foundation of belief that has sustained the Thomasine church for nearly two thousand years. However, what we and the Paulists both agree on is the Second Coming of Jesus. The Paulines have been dead wrong at every turn. Their record is perfect and unblemished. The Thomasine church itself has divided many times over the question. The Jesus is in Galilee Church was created as a result of one such division."

Swale paused to take a handkerchief from the pocket inside his suit jacket. His face was red and hot. He mopped his brow and asked if Twin Brother Osgood could go to the kitchen to fetch him a glass of water. What could I say? He still had a gun, although, by this time, he had put it in the side pocket of his jacket. Osgood returned with the water and Swale took a polite gulp and then continued with his rap.

"The Jesus is in Galilee Church believes Jesus Christ has returned to earth and has walked among us."

"Hallelujah!" said Twin Brother Osgood.

"That is the good news, Mr. Toast. Jesus has returned to save humanity and cleanse the world of its sins and to wash us all in the blood of the lamb."

I shuddered. "That sounds disgusting. That last part."

Swale ignored me. He looked to be one gear away from rapture.

"Yes, it is miraculous. Jesus Christ has walked among men in our lifetime. Yet, as it was in His own Last Times, He has been denied, ridiculed and persecuted. But the brothers and sisters of our church are spreading the good news. We are sharing the revelation that Jesus Christ has returned and the Kingdom of God is at hand." Reverend Swale mopped his brow again and smiled. "Isn't it wonderful, Mr. Toast?"

"Im afraid to ask. Who is Jesus this time around? I don't think he's made the newspapers under his own name. At least not the *COMET*."

Reverend Swale and Twin Brother Osgood looked at each other and grinned. "I thought you knew," Swale said. "Jesus Christ has returned to earth as Elvis Presley."

Chapter 17

I should have seen it coming, but I didn't. They knew my name, they had guns and hadn't I just spent three days with a guy talking about the King of Rock and Roll? However, the religious stuff was a big knuckleball. I didn't know how to play that one.

But Swale wasn't finished. He switched gears and went on to talk about Elvis and the Colonel. He did let me take that pee and get dressed. I felt he was going to be a while. So, Jan would have to wait. That was cool. Nobody in LA shows up on time anyway. It is considered bad manners.

"The similarities between Jesus and Elvis are inescapable," Swale said, when I returned to the living room. He was speaking faster than before and his voice seemed to have risen a full octave. He was beginning to sound a lot like Coates and that made me squirm. "Both Jesus and Elvis had twin brothers. They say Elvis' twin died at birth, but we wonder."

"We wonder," echoed Twin Brother Osgood.

"Jesus was born of Joseph and Miriam."

"Miriam?" I repeated.

"The real name given to Mary. Elvis was born of Vernon and Gladys. All four names have six letters each. And each twin has eleven letters each. Judas Thomas and Jesse Garron. There are other revealing signs. Elvis believed in the power of numbers. Not astrology, but the numerology as found in the Old Testament. The number 24 was a very important number to Elvis. In secular numerology the number 24 means 'fortunate' and promises assistance and association to those of high rank and position. It also represents the sum total of letters in the names Miriam, Joseph, Gladys and Vernon, the holy parents.

"Now, Mr. Toast, consider the date of Elvis' so-called death—August 16th. August is the eighth month. Add to this the date—16—and what do you get? Twenty Four. Then add 1977, the year of his so-called death and you come up with 2001."

"Stanley Kubrick!" I said, reflexively.

"Correct. *2001: A Space Odyssey.* 'Thus Spake Zarathustra' was the film's theme music, if you will remember. It was also Elvis' theme song. Coincidence? We think not. It is a clue. In 1977 Elvis Presley was 42 years-old. Jesus could have been as old as 42 when he went to the cross."

"Another coincidence?" I asked.

"Don't you see? August 16, 1977 was the only date Elvis could 'die' if he was the Lord. If he was simply an overweight drugged-up rock and roll singer, he could have died anytime. But the evidence is there. The evidence that Elvis Presley is Jesus Christ returned. It took his death to proclaim him messiah, just as it had done nearly two thousand years ago."

Reverend Swale moved to the edge of his seat. His enthusiasm was only equaled by his rapturous smile. He seemed to truly believe what he was saying, or at least he wanted me to believe that he truly believed what he was saying. That's the sign of a good evangelist. He paused only long enough to take another sip of water.

"It was a brilliant choice," he said, "that Jesus chose to return in a form that would put him in a position to lead the masses. Elvis Presley was the most recognized man on the planet. His fans numbered into the tens of millions. He was the King of Kings returned as the King of Rock and Roll. He was planning to transform his music career into the messianic ministry He had led in Israel during the Last Times. And just as He fulfilled the prophecies of the Old Testament by going to the cross, He, as Elvis, would have to die and be born again in order to become the proclaimed messiah in our own times."

"Let me get this straight," I interrupted. "Are you saying Elvis faked his own death?"

"Jesus Christ as Elvis appeared to die in order that we could all be reborn in the bosom of the Father. Just as the cross on Golgotha did not kill Jesus, a drug overdose in Memphis did not take the life of Elvis Presley."

"This just gets weirder, doesn't it? They did bury someone at Graceland, didn't they?"

"I have saved the best for last," he said, waving his right arm, the way television preachers do. "Elvis Presley left three very obvious clues at his so-called death scene. The power of the number three. The clues were books. Three books."

Swale held out the forefinger of his left hand and pushed it back with the forefinger of his right. "first," he said, "was *Cheiro's Book of Numbers*." He stuck out his middle finger and bent it back with the forefinger of his right hand. "Second was *The Mystery of the Shroud of Turin*." He extended the ring finger of his left hand and bent it back. "And third, there was a copy of *The Passover Plot*. The last book was found in the same room with the body."

Okay, so there were three books. Maybe even interesting books, especially *The Passover Plot*, the book that speculates Jesus staged and survived his own crucifixion. But clues? Anyone could have had those three books. However, Reverend Thurley Swale was on the freight train of faith. It made no stops, this train.

He continued to heap coal into the boiler. "And if these clues aren't enough for the skeptical, the circumstances surrounding Elvis' so-called death and burial should be conclusive, even for a doubter such as yourself."

"To tell you the truth, I didn't follow Elvis all that

closely."

"The time of 'death', the cause of 'death', the weight of the 'body', the mishandled police and coroner's report, the missing files and the death certificate have all been changed, destroyed or obscured to such a degree that it is obvious a cover-up was in process from the moment Elvis departed this earth."

Twin Brother Osgood sat up in his chair. "Don't forget to tell him about the casket, Twin Brother Thurley."

"Patience, brother," Swale said, without looking at him. "The police closed the case at 8:10 p.m., a mere six hours after the 'body' was discovered at Graceland and taken to a funeral home owned by a family friend. Although Elvis weighed nearly 250 pounds, the body removed from Graceland was entered on the death certificate as weighing 170 pounds."

I nodded toward Twin Brother Osgood. "What's this about the body in the casket?"

"The casket weighed an incredible 900 pounds. The body was only viewed by close friends and associates. Elvis' father let slip the remark that the body in the coffin was not that of his son."

"Oh?"

"We think it was a wax dummy cooled by an air conditioning unit. That would explain the great weight of the casket." Swale paused and took another sip of water.

I slapped my knees and stood up. "Well, this has been most interesting, reverend. I suppose you want me to write it up for the *COMET*? Well, you've got it." I looked at my watch. "Now, if you will excuse me, I am late for—"

"Sit down, Mr. Toast!" Swale's words were in the form of an order. In case I had any doubts, he reached into his jacket pocket and fingered the gun. I sat down. To hell with Jan.

"Elvis Presley IS Jesus Christ returned to save mankind. He staged His own death just as Jesus did. And He planned to return just as Jesus planned to return. However, something happened that prevented

111

Jesus' return. And something has happened that has delayed the second return. Do you know what has prevented the Second Coming in both cases?" I shook my head. I thought it might have been a trick question.

Swale stood up. His shoulders rose and he pounded his fist. "Paul!" he shouted. "The apostate from the Law and his satanic teachings. He made it impossible for Jesus to return to his ministry for the reasons I mentioned earlier. He defamed and poisoned the teachings of Jesus and built a church based on a false Jesus. The anti-Jesus. The same thing has happened with Elvis. This time Paul has taken the form of his artistic agent."

"That would be Colonel Parker," I said with a start.

"The evil agent of Satan himself. Colonel Thomas Parker, thief, carnival con man, deceitful opportunist and obscene merchandiser of Elvis Presley's death. He is the twentieth century's Saul of Tarsus. The man who has poisoned the waters and made a hundred fortunes licensing icons and shrines of the dead messiah. This is exactly the way Paul profited from the 'death' of Jesus." Swale was sweating. He took off his jacket and mopped his brow with his hankie.

"You're serious about this, aren't you?" I said, still trying to figure out the nature of the show being played in my front room.

Swale ignored me. "The day Elvis died, Colonel Parker called Harry Geissler, president of Factors, the giant merchandising company to negotiate the Elvis Presley souvenir rights. He made a second call to Vernon Presley to make sure he made no deals with outsiders who might want to exploit the Elvis Presley name. That was something Parker reserved for himself. For the first five years after Elvis' so-called death, Parker froze Elvis' family out of most of the money that came to the Presley estate. He was the sole merchandiser of Elvis' life and work. Parker's parallel to Paul is horrifying. It has only been in recent years that Parker's stranglehold on Elvis Presley has begun to relax. But it is still not time for Him to return."

"When will the time be right?" I didn't mean to

sound sarcastic, but it was inherent in the question?

"Soon, Mr. Toast, soon."

"Soon," repeated Twin Brother Osgood.

Swale finished the water in his glass. "The Church of Jesus is in Galilee has a mission. Our mission is to clear the way for His return. We have exposed Colonel Parker for what he is and daily we spread the word about the meaning of the crucifixion and the overdose in Memphis. And we are making progress, Mr. Toast. Glorious progress! The good news peals like a bell in the chapel. It is being heard in the Valley of Man. But we need help to help Jesus, Mr. Toast."

Swale was pacing in a small arc in front of me. He was in his televangelist mode. I thought he was going to hold up a toll-free telephone number and ask me for a "love offering."

"We need help in the war against the forces of Satan. Satan is wily, Mr. Toast. He is devious and well-organized and heavily financed. He has prevailed on this earth for nearly two thousand years. But I am here to tell you that with your help, Satan's days are numbered!"

"What the heck can I do?"

"The satanic descendants of Paul want the world to believe that Elvis Presley died in a bathroom in Memphis. They want us to believe he died of a drug overdose and that was it. However, some of the more clever of Satan's minions, Paul's direct spawn, have concocted elaborate theories about the death of Elvis Presley. They want people to believe that he was murdered by our own dear government. I told you they were clever, Mr. Toast. Clever and deceitful. They want the great American people to believe that Elvis Presley—Jesus the Lord—was murdered by the hand of the Central Intelligence Agency. They want *you* to believe that, Mr. Toast!"

"Ah," I said, leaning back in the sofa. I could feel the air escaping from my lungs. It was the other shoe that I had been waiting for. It had taken its own sweet time to drop, but drop it did. Like a steel-toed Doc

113

Martin boot. Reverend Swale and Twin Brother Osgood could not have missed the look on my face.

"We are here to tell you the truth," Swale said. "And to win you away from Satan's word delivered by one of his craftiest emissaries. An emissary that can be tied directly to Colonel Parker himself."

"And if I can't be won?" I said, testing the water.

Swale looked at Twin Brother Osgood. Osgood moved to the edge of his chair. Swale slid his hand into his coat pocket, He made sure I saw him do it.

"The days of the antichrist are numbered," Swale said after what seemed like a long silence. "I hope that yours are not, also. The truth will not be stopped. Not by anyone. We are a terrible swift sword in the army of Jesus Christ."

He hadn't mentioned Coates by name, but he didn't have to. We both knew who he was talking about. He had that knowing look in his eye that implied he knew the details of Coates' death, but I could have been projecting. Coates said the CIA was after him, not a religious cult.

Then Swale came to the payoff. "This falsifier of the Word and Saracen accomplice of the false prophet Parker has stolen a sacred object, Mr. Toast. I think you know what I am talking about."

I shrugged my shoulders in ignorance. Swale's eyes narrowed. They seemed to burn.

"We want it back, Mr. Toast. If you can help us, you will be rewarded handsomely."

I shrugged again. "I really don't have a clue to what you are talking about. Honestly!"

Swale smiled the way they do in his profession. It had the sincerity of a Jim Bakker grin. He looked at Twin Brother Osgood and nodded. They rose simultaneously and walked out of my apartment without saying another word. I looked at my watch. I was already ten minutes late for my lunch with Jan.

Chapter 18

Los Angeles has been the American capital of kooks, occult practitioners, professional cranks and religious sects since the early 1900s when a disciple of the "Purple Mother" came to Hollywood and established Krotona, a Moorish-Egyptian occult temple and set up the Esoteric School and Temple of the Rosy Cross.

Since that time the fertile Southland soil has bred and nurtured the likes of Sister Aimee and her Four Square Gospel, the New Thought movement, the Mighty I Am, a praying-for-dollars hype invented by a failed stock promoter from Chicago, the Mazdaznan Cult and Mankind United, which in the 1930s had a membership of 250,000 Southlanders, many of whom were suckered into surrendering their souls and savings in a futile attempt to eradicate war and poverty. There has also been the Agabeg Occult Church, Sanford the food scientist, the Self-Realization Fellowship of America, the Maharishi and the Manson Family. The list, like the summer in LA, is endless.

Why do they come to Los Angeles? Good question. One theory is that the City of Angels is the last stop in America. When the cults and the con men get chased out of the east, they flee west. It is the underside of the westering of America. Not only is LA the last geographical stop in the country, it is a haven. A safe house for

115

the weird. For, if nothing else, Los Angeles has evolved into a synonym for "freedom." It is the place where anything goes. Freedom from heritage, structure, convention and the past. Freedom to do anything. The last frontier for the pioneers of scam, vulgarity and whacko movements to save souls and make a buck. The place of no explanations necessary. The downtown of just do it. Los Angeles was the first city to say to hell with it. It is the place other cities secretly want to be, but don't have the nerve to admit it. Instead, they smirk and never pass up an opportunity to denounce LA as the nowhere city, the country's largest open air mental asylum, the world's largest freeway off-ramp and a hundred other epithets, all of which are correct, of course, but other cities are jealous of LA's spirit of freedom, just the same. The kooks, the cults and the cranks are the price you pay for freedom here. It's a high price, but most times I don't mind. Hey, this is why the *COMET* is located in LA. Most of my stories come from the Southland.

However, most of my stories don't involve gun-carrying religious strangefellows who threaten my life. That's what Reverend Swale did. All that balloon juice about the devil's days being numbered and a terrible swift sword in the army of Christ was just a nice way of telling me to give him what he wanted or get my ticket to heaven canceled. Like permanently.

I did some thinking about the reverend and his threats as I drove west on Santa Monica Boulevard toward Century City and lunch with Jan. I took the man seriously. Christians who make threats of force can often be counted on to back them up. That's the way the Crusades started.

In so many words, Swale said Coates had stolen some "sacred" object. He didn't say what the object was, but he seemed convinced that I had it, or at least knew what it was and where it could be found. I didn't on all counts, unless what he was after was something specific, like a document or a photo that proved Elvis was really dead. But I could only speculate on that.

116

The more I thought about it the more my head hurt. And if I had tried to figure out the theology Reverend Swale was pushing at me, I might have gone right up the spout. Jesus Christ returned to earth as Elvis Presley! It sounded like the sort of story Sherm Bolivia would suck out of his thumb. But, hey, the world is full of strange religions. If a large group of West Indians can sit around smoking twelve-inch joints and pray to a god who was a tiny Ethiopian dictator who died in the 1970s, then I guess guys in suits who call each other "twin brother" can believe Elvis Presley is Jesus. I looked at my watch. It was going on two o'clock.

Century City is located between Beverly Hills and West LA. That's the easy part. Just what it is, is something else. A fortress of glass and steel. An updated movie set of Fritz Lang's *Metropolis*. A forest of pre post-modern buildings with windows you can't see in. Banks, insurance company headquarters, condominiums and yuppie shopping malls. It is a place where money is made at alarming rates, multi-million dollar deals packaged, buyouts leveraged, cocaine snorted from jewel-gilded mirrors and the price of admission to movies is eight bucks. It's a place where you see even fewer people on the streets than in other parts of greater LA. You don't even see many cars. People drive right into the buildings and stay there until they drive back out. Century City is a mysterious place. Mysterious to me. So much concrete and so few citizens. A ghost town in glass.

Garbo's is one of those nouveau California restaurants. Lots of orange wedges, gay waiters and indoor trees. It is a place where you can spend a week's wages for dinner and a couple of drinks. That is, if you have a good job. It is a hangout for Southland glitterati. I saw a story about it on *PM Magazine*

It took me fifteen more minutes to find Garbo's once I got to Century City. It was tucked away on the mezzanine of one of the malls. It was just beyond the marble pillars of Daltry's of Beverly Hills. Daltry's the

117

furrier. It sells mink coats to millionaires who live in a
climate that rarely dips below 70 degrees fahrenheit.
Maybe that's why the air conditioned temperature in
Century City malls is a year-round 55.

Jan was sitting in a rattan chair under a ficus sipping something pink that had an umbrella in it. It was
a small umbrella. When she saw me approaching, she
looked at her watch and twisted her face into a first
class pout. She stood up and took a step toward me.
She threw her arms around my neck and gave me a
small kiss on the cheek.

"Steve, darling," she said. "It is so good to see you."
She broke her embrace and looked at her watch again.
"Did I say one-ish or two-ish? I can't remember."

"I'm late. Two guys from God showed up at my
place with guns and talked my ears off for an hour."

"Honestly," Jan said, skeptically. "I see you still
have a vivid imagination when it comes to making
excuses."

"It's true. What can I say?"

"It used to bore me." She looked at her watch for a
third time. "No matter. You are here and that's what
counts. How have you been, Steve? You look great. I
have missed you, you know. Really, it's true."

"I'm okay," I grunted. "If you don't count those
armed men of the Lord."

We sat down and a waiter came up to the table.
"Steve, what are you drinking? Get anything you want
the tab is on me."

I'm not an old fashioned guy. If a woman wants to
buy me a drink or anything else, I let her. But Jan's
offer to buy me a drink was more of a public announce-
ment. She made her offer in a voice that could have
been heard by everyone in the solarium at Garbo's.
That included the people sitting near the orangerie
where squwaking birds from foreign countries drown
out normal conversation.

"I'll have a mineral water," I said.

"You sure that's all you want? Don't let the price of
the drinks scare you off. This is a very spendy place,

but don't worry, I'm loaded."

"Okay. I'll have a mineral water with a twist of the most expensive lemon in the house." The waiter rolled his eyes and clicked his teeth. Jan looked at her glass.

"I'll have another one of these divine pink things," she said. The waiter left. I looked past Jan to the nearby fountain and the lily pads floating around the artificial pond.

"So," Jan said, wearing a wide smile. "Here we are again. Toast and Jan. Just like old times."

"Just like old times," I repeated. I picked up the large, hand-lettered menu. "What do you recommend? I've never been to this joint before."

Jan picked up her menu and began scanning the entrees. "Well," she said, in that LA voice that tries to make the exotic sound ordinary. "If you are interested in appetizers, I'd go for the baby artichoke and anchovy tart."

"I hate anchovies."

"Oh, sorry. I forgot."

"It's okay, I don't want an appetizer."

"I'm paying, Steve, Get anything you want. Go wild."

"What I want is no appetizer."

"Okay. You've made your point. Now, let's see." She returned to studying the menu. "Garbo's is famous for its Cal-Mex cuisine. It's all very good. Last time I was here I had the Chilean sea bass taco. It was primo. The shrimp tamales are very good. How about the duck-stuffed chile rellenos?"

"You order for me, Jan. Anything will do. I lost my appetite in restaurant food when hamburgers broke the six dollar barrier."

"Well, don't sound so enthusiastic."

"Okay, I'll watch it."

"Still the comedian, Steve."

"Take my wife, please." I smiled a thin, watery smile. Jan buried her face in the menu.

Jan ordered for both of us. I got the Chilean sea bass taco or the duck rillenos, I can't remember which. Diane

119

Keaton came into the solarium. At least that's what I heard the people at the next table say. Whoever it was, she created quite a head-turning buzz. I looked, but couldn't spot a knit hat in the place.

By the time the food came I had found my happy face and put it on. I told Jan how good she looked and how far she had come since the days when we were something of an item. I did my level best to sound sincere, but it had the gilt of tinsel, the stuff that built this town. We chatted about mutual friends and the places we used to go. I was almost enjoying myself. And Jan did look good. Real good.

"Remember the time," I said, waxing nostalgic, "you dropped your sno-cone down the back of that fat lady on Olvera Street?" Jan giggled and nodded her head. "I thought her husband was going to kill me. You did that on purpose, didn't you? Drop the sno-cone down that lady's back."

"*Moi?*" Jan said, feigning innocence.

"I seem to remember we were arguing about where to go for dinner."

"I remember saving your life from the woman's husband."

"Yeah. I thought he was going to strangle me with his polyester belt. Did I ever say thanks?"

"Later that night. I think you said thank you three times. You wore me out." We both giggled. I felt the urge to hold her hand, but fought it off.

"So," she said, after an uneasy pause. "Here we are. Toast and Jan." She always liked saying that. It was her biggest concession to humor in the three years we were together.

"Yeah. Toast and Jan."

"So, what were you doing at the *Times* library last night? Dickstein said you were there for a long time."

"Nothing really. Just checking on some things."

"Big story? I know you've got some big stories in you, Steve. I've always said that."

"Just some stuff. Hardly worth mentioning."

"Oh, come on, Steve. You're too modest. I've always said that, too. You've got so much talent. It's a shame to see it wasted."

"You always said that, too. Let's change the subject."

"I'm interested in you, Steve. I'm interested in your work. What are you up to? Something top secret? You can trust me."

"Just some stuff I'm doing for the *COMET*. You know, the old 'World War II Bomber Found on the Moon' stuff."

"I don't believe that for a minute. Whatever I may think of the *COMET*, I know you have too much integrity to make up a story."

"Maybe I've changed."

"Dickstein said you were looking at clips on Elvis Presley." I looked Jan straight in the eye when she said that. I was looking for a visual sneer or at least some condescension. I found no signs of either.

"Well, you found me out. I'm an Elvis nut. You didn't know that about me, did you? Why do you think I let my sideburns grow?" I pointed to my sideburns, whose length are boringly normal.

Jan laughed once. "You never take yourself seriously, do you, Steve?"

I looked around. "It's hard to in a place like this."

"Well, I *am* interested in your work. What's your spin on Elvis?"

"Just poking around. No spin, no story."

"Come on, Steve. This is Jan you're talking to, not a rival journalist from another tabloid out to scoop you."

"Then you are not speaking as the LA bureau chief of the Washington *Post*?"

"Of course not. I'm your friend. Besides, the *Post* isn't interested in Elvis Presley, dead or alive."

"Then you think he's dead?"

"Yes, don't you?"

"I don't know. There seems to be some doubt about that."

"Are you serious?"

"I don't know about that, either."

"You're speaking in riddles."

"I know."

"What on earth would possess you to spend half the night in the *Times* library reading clips about Elvis Presley? Dickstein said you also pulled some files on the CIA. Is there a connection?"

"Dickstein is a very nosy person."

"He's a journalist. It's his job to be nosey."

"He's nosey and it's his job to be a journalist."

"You haven't answered my question. Is there a connection between Elvis and the CIA?" Jan tilted her head to one side and giggled. "I can see the headline in the *COMET*—'Elvis the Singing Spy'."

"Maybe."

"You are so evasive, Steve. You would think you had been the first journalist to discover that Nixon ordered the Watergate cover-up."

"What do you know about the Jesus is in Galilee Church?"

"My God! You haven't found religion, have you, Steve?"

"The two guys with the guns. They said that was the name of their church."

"What are you talking about?"

"They were interested in Elvis, too. More important than that, they were interested in my interest in Elvis."

"Meaning?" The tone of Jan's voice dropped ten degrees.

"Meaning nothing other than a lot of people are getting twisted out of shape over a rock and roll singer who has been dead going on fifteen years."

"I am not getting twisted out of shape."

"I didn't necessarily mean you, Jan."

"I hope not. We can drop the subject if you like. I have something much more important to discuss."

"Like?"

"Like how would you like a job with the Washington *Post?*

Chapter 19

I thought about the Dodgers on my way in to the
COMET. Specifically, I thought about Don Drysdale
and Orel Hershiser and all those consecutive shutout
innings they pitched. Nearly sixty innings each without
giving up a single run. Now that really takes belief in
yourself. That, plus a whole lot more, like a good fast-
ball, a curve that breaks at right angles and a catcher
who knows what pitch to call and when.

I always liked to think I was the Drysdale and
Hershiser of gutter journalism. Nobody could get anything by me. My dream image of myself was that of a
lean, mean, don't-try-any-shit-on-me machine. A guy
who could take to the mound and strike out the side
just because he was the guy who could do it. One cynical mother. Invincible, like Don and Orel.

However, the last few days had seen the armor
crack. Doubt had beat out an infield hit and confusion
had stroked a double off the left field wall. Then Jan
asked me to go to work for the Washington *Post*. That
was a base-clearing shot into the upper deck. Steve
Toast was no longer the record-setting cynical shutout
ace of the Southland. No trip to the Hall of Fame for
him. He had been turned into a palooka in just three
days and was on his way down to the minor leagues.

Jan sounded serious when she made her offer. But
then Jan always sounded serious about everything. She

told me she was authorized by her boss in D.C. to hire me to work in the LA bureau. She said she had shown him some of my old clips and he was impressed. All that and $60,000 a year. I asked Jan to give me a couple of days to think about it. She was disappointed that I didn't take a flying leap at it right there in Garbo's, but agreed to give me two days. She said she would make dinner at her place the day after tomorrow. I didn't verbally commit, but Jan told me to be at her place in Westwood at eight o'clock sharp. It was the same thing as making a verbal commitment.

I got to the *COMET* at four. There was a message on my desk to see Barfyskowicz the minute I arrived. It had the tone of a ransom note. I went straight to his office. The door was open. I walked in. The Barfman started barking before I reached his desk.

"Son of a bitch, Toast! Where the hell have you been? I've been busting my lumps all day trying to reach you. I'm holding next week's front page for your Elvis story. I hope to God you've got some juice to lay on me."

"Hi, Stan."

"Fuck 'hi, Stan'. You got some juice for me, or what? The publisher has been climbing up my ass. He wants something and he wants it last week. He's one bad hombre and I can't hold him off forever. He's threatened to fire every one of our white asses if circulation doesn't pick up. He's talking a million and he's talking this month. That's a million increase! So, don't tell me 'hi, Stan.' Tell me something that will calm my bowels."

I sat down in the chair in front of his desk. "Stan," I said, trying to calm his bowels. "What I've got is big. Real big, but...."

Barfyskowicz slammed his hand on the desk. A jar of pens keeled over. "I knew it! goddamnit, I just knew it! My ass is hay. And yours, too, Mr. College Graduate."

"Hold on, Stan."

The Barfman ran a hand through his thinning

124

hair. He looked like a man in need of a horse-sized tranquilizer."

"Deep Coates is dead," I said, getting right to the point.

The Barfman's eyes grew as large as hockey pucks and his mouth ripped out a grin. "That's great! What a lead." He paused and frowned. "It wasn't natural causes, was it?"

"Relax. You will be pleased to know there is a good chance he was murdered."

"Fantastic! Who did it? You think the little shit was on the level about the CIA?"

"You're amazing, you know that, Stan?"

"Hold the compliments for later, Toast. I want details on how the little squirrel was popped."

I shook my head. "He wasn't a little squirrel. Or a little shit. He was a human being."

The Barfman made an obscene gesture with his eyes. "Save your bleeding heart for the liberal ladies garden club. I run a newspaper, not a grief counseling service."

"Right. How stupid of me to forget."

"So, get to the bottom rung, Toast. When can I have part one of your blockbuster series?"

"I'll need at least a week."

"Impossible! You've got two days and not a minute more. You blow this, Toast and you're shit-canned. That's the word from up high. The man told me he'd fire me if I didn't deliver. I can't deliver if you don't deliver. You don't deliver and I'll see to it that you'll never write another line for any tabloid in this country."

"I'm confused. Is that a threat or a promise?"

"Get out of here, Toast! I don't want to see your white ass until I have your story on my desk. I'm putting Sherm on the story to work with you. He got wind of it and practically insisted. But he will be an asset. Use him. He knows Elvis better than anyone around here. You can use Braska, Bubblefarb, anyone you want to work with you. Two days, Toast. Two mother-grabbing days!" The Barfman wiped the lather from his lips and down-shifted. "You will have a story for old Stan, won't you, Steve? I'm counting on you, good buddy. You're the best I've got. By God, if anyone can do it, you can. Can I have your word that you can do it?"

"I'll have something for you, Stan."

"That's my boy."

"Unless I turn up on a slab at the morgue or working for the *Post*."

"Huh? The *Post*? What are you talking about? Is this another one of your little jokes?"

"Yeah, I guess it could be."

"Well, cut the comedy. This is serious business. You've got work to do. I'm counting on you, Toast. Don't let the team down. Go out there and win one for the Barfman." My eyebrows snapped to attention. "You didn't think I knew what you guys call me behind my back, did you? Well, nothing gets by the Barfman. Remember that, Toast."

"Right. I'll try to win one for the Barfman."

"Yeah. Now get out of here, I've got things to do."

I walked back to my desk. I passed Shelly Bubblefarb on the way. She was carrying a bag of fresh ground coffee. I could smell it. She wrinkled her nose when she saw me like I was a bad smell at the beach. She said something as we passed each other. It was more of a mumble. It didn't sound like "hello."

Sherman Bolivia was sitting at my desk when I returned. He had a look on his face that told me he'd been waiting for me and had probably gone through my desk drawers just to pass the time.

"Sherm," I said. "What's up?"

He grinned, but it wasn't a friendly grin. "Your ass, if I hear right." Then the grin on Sherm's face dropped like a cheap souffle. "What the hell are you doing writing Elvis stories? That's what I want to know. I thought you were just making talk the other day. I didn't know you were writing a goddamned article. A goddamned series! You!"

"It wasn't my idea, Sherm. The Barfman dumped it

126

in my lap. What was I supposed to do?"

"You could have come to me and said, 'Sherman, the Barfman has given me a story to do on Elvis. I know Elvis is your area of expertise and I have no doubt you would do a far better job with it, but that's life. I humbly ask you to forgive me for scabbing on your turf'."

"That would have satisfied you?"

"Hell, no, but you could have groveled. I would have groveled for you, Toast."

"You're a real *mensch*, Sherm."

"Forget it. What have you got so far? It might not be too late for me to save your ass and the story." Sherm took out a pair of glasses from his shirt pocket and put them on. It was his way of telling me the professionals had been called in to do the job right. I humored him up to a point.

I told him about Coates and a good part of his tale about the CIA action to kill Elvis. Sherm just shook his head. I told him about the tapes I had made of the Coates interviews, but I didn't tell him that I had found Coates dead in his bed. I also told him about Reverend Swale and the Jesus is in Galilee Church, but nothing about the guns and threats.

I don't know why I held back Coates' death and the guns part. It just seemed like the right thing to do. Like something the smart detectives do in mystery novels. I was neither a detective, nor particularly smart— smart in the way detectives are smart— but I held back some of the important stuff anyway. Maybe it was the newspaper man in me. I had worked hard for what I had gathered on the Elvis story. I didn't feel right spooning it to Bolivia like jell-o from a bowl. I felt obliged to make him work for whatever he got. It would be a fresh experience for him.

"Why couldn't the CIA have killed Elvis?" I said, trying to change the direction of the flow of information.

Sherm was irritated by the question. "The government doesn't go around killing rock and roll singers, that's why."

"Well, I don't know. They say somebody had Otis Redding killed."

"Jesus, Toast! You're starting to believe the crap you write. I'm telling you, Elvis Presley was a hillbilly rock star who took every drug in the pharmaceutical almanac. It was only a question of time before he overdosed or mixed the wrong drugs."

"Simple as that, eh?"

"Simpler. Just cut out this CIA crap. You know we're not political here. Besides, it won't fly, despite what the Barfman says. The publisher would kill it. Take it from me, he's a personal friend of mine.The publisher. I'm telling you, Toast, you're asking for nothing but trouble if you try to make it a political thing."

"I'm already in trouble."

"The religious angle is better. Could be great stuff. A religious cult that believes Elvis is Jesus. Yeah, that one's got legs. It could walk us into the sunshine, Toast. What did you say the name of that church was?"

"The Jesus is in Galilee Church."

"Great. You think you could talk to them again?"

"I think I can count on it."

"Fantastic. Tell you what we do. We set up a meeting with them. I'll try to get a cameraman. We could use some good photos. Maybe we can go to one of their church services. Yeah, that's what we should do. I got a guy who feeds me stuff on the occult and religious nuts. I'll call him to get a line on these bozos."

I nodded. It was a perfunctory nod. The look in Sherm's eyes and the tone of his voice told me he was going to do what he wanted. Whether or not I agreed was of no particular consequence to him. If, by chance, I had happened to miss the meaning of the look and tone, he told me flat out in his own words.

"I'm willing to bail your ass out on this, Toast," he said. "But I'm telling you right up front, I get a by-line." Again I nodded perfunctorily. "First thing I want to do is listen to those tapes."

"I thought you said the CIA angle was scrap city?"

"Yeah, but I want to hear them anyway. You never know. I might be able to salvage something out of them."

"What a prince."

"Hey, if you'd have come to me in the first place, you wouldn't be in all this deep shit. Now, when can you get the tapes to me? You got them here?" His eyes opened my desk drawers.

"No. They're at home."

"We'll kill two birds with one stone. I'll call my guy and if he has something for me, I'll see if we can go to this church to see the Jesus freaks in action. You can bring the tapes with you when you come."

"I don't know."

"Jesus, Toast! I'm trying to save your ass. Look alive, pal. We don't have much time. I'll get back to you this evening. You going to be home?"

"Yeah, I think so,"

"Good." Sherm slapped his knees and stood up. "Okay. Got to get to work." He put a hand on my shoulder. "We'll get something going on this, Toast. You can count on Sherman Bolivia to come through in the clutch."

"Yeah. Give me a call tonight if you turn up anything."

Bolivia turned and walked away. I sat at my desk staring at my framed team picture of the '90 Dodgers trying to remember all of the names.

I left for home twenty minutes later. I saw Sherm at his desk talking on the phone as I walked through the city room. He nodded to me. I nodded back. I continued through the news room toward the elevator. My head turned to the red-flocked wallpaper of Armitage Shanks' salon. Try not turning your head when you see red-flocked velvet wallpaper. I saw Armitage and Randy sipping tea.

Armitage waved when he saw me. I waved back. But this was not the wave of greeting. It was a "come here" wave. I detoured into Armitage's salon.

"Dear boy," he said, sounding like a character from

129

Masterpiece Theatre. "I've been desperate to speak to you all day."

I looked toward the elevator. "Well, I'm sort of on my way out of here, Armitage."

"In more ways than one, dear boy, if the grapevine bears true fruit."

"What? Did the Barfman hold a staff meeting and drag my butt through it for all to enjoy?"

"*Au contraire.*" Armitage put his fingers to his lips. "This is *entre nous.*" He looked at Randy. "Randy, be a dear and run to the store. We're nearly out of biscuits." Randy rose and left without saying a word.

"The English call their cookies biscuits, you know," Armitage said. "It has a certain ring to it, don't you think? I mean, cookies are for children. Biscuits are for discerning adults."

"Yeah, right. You haven't been waiting all day to tell me that, have you, Armitage?"

He laughed and covered his mouth with the tips of his fingers. "You are the funny one. No, dear boy, I am afraid what has come to these old ears is a bit more serious than what name to call baked dough sweets."

"I'll save you the trouble. I got it straight from the Barfman himself not an hour ago."

"What I have heard goes beyond our esteemed editor's rantings, I am afraid."

"What are you talking about?"

"Remember when you asked me if Elvis Presley could be alive?"

"You spoke to James Dean?"

"Dear boy, this is serious."

"Sorry."

"It seems that our dearly departed Mr. Sideburns may no longer be counted among the living, but some of his possessions still are."

"What do you mean?"

"People collect anything. Bottle caps, rare books, match book covers. I had an uncle who collected different kinds of tree bark. An odd chap, but completely harmless. He had a very large collection as I remember.

130

Filthy bits of bark all over his house. I remember my aunt complaining to mother about it."

"Armitage!"

"Yes. The point being, dear boy, Elvis memorabilia is one of the hottest collectibles on the market today. I understand some of the most inane props from those dreadful films he made fetch five and six figures."

"What has this got to do with me?"

"I have heard it upon the most reliable of authorities that one of the biggest Elvis collectors in the land turned up dead recently and that you might have been the last person to have seen him alive."

"Coates!" I gasped the name without thinking. That explained the museum at his house. It didn't explain much else, but it did raise a lot of questions. Like how did Armitage find out I visited Coates the day of his death.

"Yes," he said, taking a sip from his tea cup. "I believe that was the chap's name. What concerns you dear boy, is the pickle you seem to be in as a result of your association with your Mr. Coates."

"I didn't kill him."

Armitage squeezed off a small laugh. "Dear boy, that is a secondary worry. No, my sources tell me that a priceless, what shall we call it—*object d'Elvis* was thought to be in the late Mr. Coates' possession at the time of his demise. Certain other Elvis collectors, I understand, had been negotiating the purchase of it."

"What was it?"

"I'm not very keen on collectors or collectibles. Not the obsessive-compulsive ones. They are a skin rash on the culture, as far as I'm concerned. Everything is so hush-hush in their little cloistered world. My sources were unable to ascertain the precise identity of the object. However, I am sure you can see the implication of what I am telling you."

"Someone thinks I killed Coates and stole this Elvis article?"

"Precisely."

"That would explain the guys with the guns?"

131

"I beg your pardon."

"Nothing. Who are these collectors?"

" Besotted, be-money-bagged purveyors of Elvis Presley's laundry and other detritus, I presume. My sources hear snips and snaps of things. They are not the eleven o'clock news, dear boy."

"Right."

"However, I do know something about collectors. The really big collectors. They are as obsessive as they are rich. They can collect things because they have the money to do so. Price is no object with them. However, if they can't get what they want with their wheelbarrows of cash, they have the motivation, and more importantly, the power to get it other ways."

"Meaning?"

"I am sure I don't have to spell it out for you, dear boy. I am simply telling you there may be certain individuals out there who want something you have, or think you have, and I really don't think they care how they get it."

"I don't suppose you have any names?"

"Alas, no. The names of the really big collectors are rarely known to such as we."

I got to my feet to leave. "Thanks, Armitage. This has really made my day complete."

"Just a morsel of news from a friend, dear boy. And a plea to be careful out there in the big bad city." I turned to leave. "Oh, before you go gently into the night, there is something else."

I turned and faced him. He took the cup and saucer from his lap and put it on the coffee table in front of him. "I wouldn't place my trust in some of my colleagues, if I were you."

"Oh, great. Who?"

"I really don't like naming names, dear boy."

"Armitage. It's your job to name names. You are a professional gossip."

"I beg your pardon, Mr. Toast. I am a celebrity columnist." Armitage pulled on the sleeves of his shirt and extended his right hand to examine his fingernails.

"Who do you mean? Who shouldn't I trust?"

"Perhaps I have said too much already. Besides, what does the word of a professional gossip count for, anyway?"

"Christ! Armitage, please!"

"Let us simply say the initials of this colleague are 'S. B.' and leave it at that."

The phone at the side of his mohair chair rang. Armitage picked it up and began speaking. I stood my ground for a full two minutes. Armitage crossed his legs and turned away from me. My audience with Armitage Shanks had come to an end.

I took the freeway home. Or maybe I took Santa Monica Boulevard, I don't remember. My mind was on overload. I just pointed my car toward the ocean and let instinct do the rest.

"S. B." Armitage must have meant Sherm Bolivia. Sherm is a weasel, but his danger is more in obnoxious jokes and ethical poverty than in anything that might be called backstabbing. The kind of backstabbing that uses a real knife. Besides, didn't he tell me himself that he was horning in on my Elvis story for a by-line and by inference to boost his ego. The main thing to watch out for with Sherm Bolivia was that he didn't turn the story into another "Photographer Takes Picture of Heaven" Bolivia extravaganza of schlock. Still.

When I got close enough to the ocean I could smell it. Rotting kelp, dead fish and saltwater. If that smell was in a bucket it would make most people puke, but there is something about the smell of the ocean that invigorates the senses and the mind. It was my invigorated mind that realized that just about everyone I worked with had the initials S. B.—Shelly Bubblefarb, Sue Braska and Stan Barfyskowicz. In fact, Armitage Shanks was probably the only person at the *COMET* who knew I was working on the Elvis story who didn't have the initials S.B.

Chapter 20

The size of the black population in Los Angeles grew slowly. By 1920 less than three percent of the city was black. But it was a segregated town, nonetheless. The segregated areas kept moving south until they were concentrated in Watts.

There is no reason to go to Watts if you're not black, unless it is to see those weird-looking ziggurats covered with pieces of cut glass, jewelry bits and mosaic tiles they call the Watts Towers.

Watts is not your typical eastern tenement ghetto. It is mostly single-family houses, wide streets, broadleaf trees and parks. In 1964 the Urban League rated Los Angeles first among 68 American cities as the best place for black people to live. One reason for this, said some experts—both white and black—was that racial hatred toward blacks was not as pernicious in LA as it was in other cities. It wasn't the case, they said, that LA was so enlightened, but rather the long and murderous racist hatred of white Angelinos had been concentrated on Mexicans and Chinese instead.

But a ghetto is a ghetto and Watts was among the first to explode. The year was 1965. A total of 34 people were killed—31 by the police. Over 1,000 were injured and 4,000 arrested. More than 6,000 buildings were damaged or destroyed and property loss ran to 40 million dollars. America was never to be the same again after Watts. It was the end of an age of innocence that never really was.

In addition to the towers and the riots there is a third Watts. Bob Watts. Reverend Bob Watts. "Sixman." Bob Watts is a religious and community leader in the greater Watts area and he is a well-known public figure in the whole of LA. He started out as a Catholic priest but jumped ship when he found out he didn't have a very good chance of becoming Pope. He operates a small non-denominational church off Avalon, near the intersection where that policeman pulled over that car twenty-five years ago and hassled that young black guy, precipitating that incident which touched off the riots.

Next to the church is the recreation hall. It is always full of young black kids playing and dreaming of making it to the pros. During most of the year basketball is king at the center. Kareem is a frequent visitor conducting clinics or just shooting hoops with the neighborhood hot shots.

I know Bob Watts because it is hard to be in the newspaper business and not know him. Wherever he goes, whatever he does, he makes noise. A lot of noise. That is how he got the nickname "Sixman". Ask anyone who regularly attends Laker basketball games about the guy in the stands with the megaphone lungs and they will tell you he is the Lakers inspirational "sixth man".

I know Watts because he regularly phones, mails and sometimes personally delivers material to the *COMET*. Most of what he gives us is on religion. Things like miracles, fakes, spiritual experiences and sometimes controversial issues that concern the church. He is something of a scholar in the area and although most of his stuff is too smart for the *COMET*, we usually find something of his to run. Often I am the guy he talks to, whether over the phone or in person. I also like the Lakers and sometimes he'd come in and we would just talk basketball.

Watts wasn't in his office so I checked the courts outside the rec center. He was there, graying hair and all, playing one-on-one against a neighborhood teenag-

135

er who was wearing sneakers that looked like they cost more than my television set.

"Hey, Bob!" I called out.

Watts looked up. The teenager seized the moment and dribbled around the sweating minister and went straight for the basket. He scored easily.

"Damn!" Watts spit at me. "You trying to make me look bad in front of this youngster?" I shrugged my shoulders. "Toast!" he exclaimed, wiping the sweat from his brow and looking at me. "It's you." I nodded. "Toast to the post. Let's you and me go one-on-one after I teach this youth the fundamentals of the game."

"Shee-it!" said the teenager.

"Actually, I left my Nikes at home. I came to ask you something. It's got to do with religion. A church."

"Then you came to the right place, bro. Give me five minutes with this youngster."

"Five minutes and you be dead, old man," said the confident teen.

"Oh, yeah?" snapped Watts. He took the ball and drove to the basket. The teenager stayed with him. Suddenly, Watts stopped and launched a twelve-foot jump shot that sailed through the netless rim. "In your face," he gloated, playfully. "Can you keep up the pace?"

A few minutes later Watts slipped by his man for the game-winning layup. He put his arm on the teenager's shoulder and said something to him. The kid smiled. He took the ball and headed off to the other end of the court.

"Whew!" said Watts, picking up a towel from the top of his sports bag. "Another year and I won't be able to beat that kid."

"Yeah. We're all slowing down."

"Fuck slowing down! He's getting better, that's all. Last time Magic came out here, the kid nearly took him. UCLA is hot to sign him, but I think he will go to North Carolina or some other Atlantic Coast Conference school."

We started walking toward the church and his office. "Yassir," he continued, with an exaggerated drawl. "Those white gentlemens down Dixie way jes' lub our colored young'uns here in Mudtown." Watts laughed. It was a sarcastic laugh. "Yassir. They's bringin' back the plantation system, sure 'nuff. Onliest thing is, now they pays black folk for shooting baskets while their great grandmammies and pappies jes' filled 'em." His voice returned to normal. "But, hey, for the couple hundred black kids who make it, it's the sweet life. For the rest, it's just the latest version of the race's bad dream. Still, I love the game. You see the Lakers last night?"

"No, I've been out of touch the last few days. They're in the playoffs, right?"

Watts stopped in his tracks. I stopped with him. He looked at me like I had just told him I was selling atomic secrets to the Russians. "Man, I thought you were a Lakers fan."

"I am."

"Only a fool would ask that kind of question. We had seats three rows behind the Laker bench. I went with the Judds."

"Wynonna and what's her name?"

"Say what?" The Judds, man. Dorsey and Bennett. They both have churches in South Central. We play in the South LA Church League."

"Oh."

"It was slamma jamma time against the Jazz. Lakers don't win last night they go two down with the series moving to Utah. Crunch time in the Mormon zone. My man Dunleavy needs the Sixman to get Magic and Worthy jump-started in the third quarter. We were down by ten, you dig, when A. C. feeds this cross-court pass to Magic. Magic drives the lane." Reverend Watts began to pantomime the play as we walked. He dribbled an imaginary basketball.

"Magic has the Mailman hanging over him like a killer octopus. Magic goes up for the shot. The Mailman has position on him. He is going to swat the ball all the way to Catalina. At the top of his leap Magic dumps the ball off to Worthy who is driving the baseline. James goes under the rim and slams the ball over his head for the deuce. Sweet, I'm telling you, it was sweet! That was the turning point. It was only a matter of time before the Lakers put it away.

"Sorry I missed it."

We entered the church and walked to the minister's office. Watts went straight for the small refrigerator at the back of the room.

"Want something cold to drink, Toast? Root beer, Diet Pepsi, Mountain Dew?" I said no. He took a Mountain Dew from the fridge and rolled the ice cold can over his forehead several times before opening it. "Ahh," he said, after the first sip. "The next best thing to being out there on the court and whipping dudes less than half your age is the post-game cold one."

I nodded. What did I know? I never played the game and the only thing at which I could beat guys less than half my age was legally buying alcohol.

"So what brings you out to Watts, Toast? You looking to buy a home?" He laughed.

"Like I said, religion brings me here."

"Don't tell me you want to join a black church. You white folks are a trip."

"No, There were these two guys of the cloth who paid me a visit yesterday. They were packing guns."

"Damn!" he said, shaking his head playfully. "White brethren take these doctrinal issues far too seriously."

"Ever hear of an outfit called the Jesus is in Galilee Church?"

"Is this a trick question?"

"I'm serious, padre."

"The Jesus is in Galilee Church. Must be a new one. I try to keep up with that kind of stuff, you know."

"Yes. That's why I came to you."

Bob Watts smiled. "Damn! And I thought you drove all the way out here to watch me play hoops."

"How about a guy who calls himself Thurley Swale? Ever hear of him?"

"Swale. Sure. He's one of our local religious space

138

cases. He used to have a church called Brethren of the Lord, I think it was. I haven't heard anything about him in awhile. He's a kook, but he knows his stuff. He's not your run-of-the-mill carny evangelist."

"How's that?"

"Well, he's a Thomasine, for one thing."

"Yeah, he said something about that. Is that bad?"

Watts laughed. "Oh, no, on the contrary. Thomasine thought is very serious and very historically based. Not like the cable TV cranks who think the Bible is the official transcript of events from Adam and Eve through the crucifixion. They're pinheads. They wouldn't know a true question of theology if it came and rented a room from them."

"So, he's on the level?"

"I didn't say that. I said Thomasine thought was on the level."

"I don't know. I only know what I heard at gunpoint. Things like Thomas was Jesus' twin brother and the bogeyman is the Apostle Paul."

Watts smiled. "Crudely put, but something like that. At least some Thomasines think that. I've never met Swale, but I know something about the Thomasines and the other gnostic sects of the early centuries A.D. You might find this hard to believe, but I did research on the Nag Hamadi Scrolls at theology school. Actually, one of the reasons I quit the Catholics was my problem swallowing Pauline doctrine. I mean, really. You've got to be just as brain-dead as brothers Falwell and Roberts to swallow Catholic dogma. It sucks, man."

"What about Swale? He's the one I'm interested in."

"Like I said, I never met the man, but I hear about him from time to time. Come to think of it the last thing I heard—when was it, a year ago—was pretty strange, even for him."

"Like Elvis Presley is the second coming of Jesus Christ."

"Yeah, something weird like that. The guy must

have either cracked up or he's working on some kind of new con."

"Do you know anything about him? I mean personally."

"Well, a lot of the stuff I've heard is unreliable. I can't drive the lane and put up two on him. He's a flake with a long tail."

"Tail?"

"Maybe they're just air balls, Toast. I've talked to some people who swear by him. Think he's God's MVP. But that was before this Elvis phase. I think he might have fouled out on this one."

"I'm looking for background, Bob. Anything you have will be useful."

"You doing a story on him?"

"Not exactly, but he's a part of it."

"Well, I heard he started out as a missionary in Central America. He was connected with that fundamentalist sect that had so much influence over the president of Guatemala. But I also heard he was a Catholic priest in D.C. You figure it out."

"So, he was in Guatemala?"

"Some folks think so. It was a sect of pentacostals. They were very strong down there for a time. I heard Swale was all over Central America bringing the word of God and American imperialism to the peasant masses."

"Was he ever in Panama?"

"I heard that he got himself thrown out of Panama, but I could be wrong about that."

"What did he do to get expelled? Was it religion or politics?"

"I don't know. They go hand-in-hand in places like that."

"Do you think he could have been CIA?"

"Well, that would be a desperation shot on my part, Toast. I never heard he was, but I do know he was in Central America at the time the CIA was very actively trying to save Somoza and was messing in Panama the same time Uncle Sam was trying to bust Torrijo's humps. He could have been doing a lot of things besides thumping the tub for Jesus. If he was Catholic, I would say the chances of him being CIA were pretty good. That's another thing I didn't like about the Catholics."

"What was that?"

"The damn CIA is pretty much run by devout, right-wing fanatical Ivy League Catholics. I was constantly in foul trouble once I began digging into the Vietnam War. I put myself on irrevocable waivers when that whole scandal with the Vatican Bank blew up. The CIA was way in over its shorts on that one."

"What else do you know about Swale?"

"You say he pulled a gun on you?"

"In my own apartment."

"Then I'd say watch your back, brother man. The dude is an armed religious nut with far right political leanings. What more can I say? Don't try to go one-on-one with him. He'll beat you every time."

I changed my mind and decided to have a cold drink after all. The Mountain Dew was ice cold. My forehead had become hot and sweaty. I felt like rolling the cold soda can over it, but I didn't.

Chapter 21

On the way home I stopped at Ralph's for some onion rolls and meat. I loaded up on potato salad and chili-mac. I got a *Times* on the way out.

The sun was beginning to set high over Venice Beach, but I had other things on my mind. I miss more sunsets that way.

I juggled the grocery bag and newspaper to get the key into the front door lock to my apartment. It wasn't necessary, the door was open. I stepped inside. The place had been tossed like a garden salad. Couches slashed, tables overturned, books thrown around the room, the usual stuff.

I walked to the kitchen to put my meat away. The door of the refrigerator was standing open and the cupboards had been dumped. I stepped on a box of crackers.

I took out a beer and popped it open and walked back into the living room. The television looked like it was still in one piece, so I turned it on. I sat on my cushionless sofa and propped my feet up on a three-legged coffee table. A rerun of the Cosby show was just coming on. I just couldn't cut myself a break.

I didn't really watch the Cosby show. I just stared at the television screen and drank my beer. I tried to think some, but I didn't want to hurt myself. I should have been scared fluidless, but there was a problem. There were too many people out there to be scared of to make fear really meaningful. From the CIA, to obsessive Elvis collectors; to religious nuts with guns, the entire staff at the *COMET* and your everyday neighborhood criminals. They canceled each other out when it came to inspiring fear.

I just sat on the sofa and stared alternately at the television and the big white tag sewn into the sofa. You've seen them before. They say "Do not remove under penalty of law." I didn't move from my spot for the longest time. I didn't think I could even if I had wanted to. Then, gathering up as much inertia as I could, my hand shot out and ripped the tag from the couch.

"Steven Toast!" said a voice from my doorway.

I turned. "Yes."

"You're under arrest." The voice belonged to one of two men who were wearing suits with wide ties.

"For pulling off a sofa tag?" I yelped, holding the evidence in my hand. "Who are you guys? The furniture police?"

The one who spoke came over to me. He had a pair of handcuffs in his hand. "You have the right to remain silent...."

"I did it!" I interrupted him. "I yanked the goddamn tag off with my bare hands, but I didn't think it would bring the cops down on me. A citation delivered through the mail, maybe, but a bust?"

"I don't know what the hell you're talking about, sport," said the one with the handcuffs. "We're taking you in on suspicion of murder."

"Murder?"

"A man named Coates. It has has been changed from a suicide to a homicide."

"What about sofacide?" I waved the white tag in front of him.

"You're nuts," he said, escorting me to my own feet and clinking the bracelets around my wrists. I did not resist.

The cops led me to the door. The one who had done all the talking stopped and looked around the over-

turned room. He shook his head and turned to his partner. "I don't see how people can live like this."

"It's disgusting," said his partner.

Chapter 22

With the exception of its history of right-wing, hard-headed and flamboyant chiefs, the LAPD is probably not significantly different from most other big city police forces. However, it is by far the best known. Even before Sergeant Joe Friday worked the day shift out of the robbery detail in the 1950s, the LA cops were famous. Or notorious, depending on how you looked at it. If you wanted, you could go all the way back to the 1850s when Los Angeles was a dusty, murderous village known as "Hell Town." There was a killing per day in the little village that was the size of a freeway off-ramp. That's about the time the Los Angeles Rangers were organized to deal with the problem of "Mexican banditry" and nearly started a race war. In 1871, the police furnished the leaders of the mob that killed and lynched twenty Chinese.

Mack Sennett took the grim edge off the Los Angeles police with films of his seltzer-down-the-pants buffoons known as the Keystone Cops. From killers to clowns. Ah, Hollywood.

But they are still cops. The guys with the guns who brought you the Watts riot and Operation Hammer, a military adventure into the black neighborhoods that resembled the U.S. Army's village pacification program during the Vietnam War. And the whole wide world saw what the LAPD did to Rodney King. That was the real "LA Law."

Chief Gates, and Chief Parker before him, sat at the top of an army that is not accountable to civil authority. They enforced the social will of the power structure in a way that can make the security forces of a Central American dictator look like those guys in the red uniforms and big furry black hats who pose for tourist photos in front of Buckingham Palace. Ask around in Watts and South Central.

I spent nearly two hours in a police station sweat box being grilled by the two policemen who had picked me up. They had been trained on a high calorie diet of cop movies. One of them recognized me from a series I did on a police drug and burglary ring when I was working for the *Times*. It was just another reason for him to hate me and make my life miserable. To him I was a professional cop-hater and thus, not entitled to any rights, constitutional or otherwise. His name was Munich. It fit.

Munich and his partner, who was named Martinez, wanted to know everything I knew about Coates. When I tried to tell them, they thought I was crazy or an obnoxious smart aleck. Either way they didn't like it.

They wanted to know what I was doing at Coates' house the night he died. I wanted to speak with a lawyer. "Fat chance, slime bag," Munich said to me. He repeated the phrase all evening. Probably picked it up from the movies.

When I tried to tell them about Swale and his gun, Munich picked me up out of my chair and threw me to the floor. He was a big man. A big, frustrated man.

I wondered why the police were so interested in the death of a little man who was one step up from a transient. Besides, an overdose of pills looked good for the cause of death. Why weren't the police out on the streets battling drug gangs and tracking down serial killers? That's what I wanted to know and said so to Munich. Martinez had to restrain him.

It didn't fit. If Coates was murdered, a likely candidate to have bumped him off would have been the CIA. That's the way Coates had called it and though I didn't

146

live inside his paranoia, it was as plausible as anything else. More plausible. What wasn't plausible was the LAPD's interest in the case. Why would the cops reopen an apparent suicide that might lead them straight to the Central Intelligence Agency? Who was on the other end pushing? Don't these guys coordinate their stuff? Maybe this was a CIA plan to get rid of me. Coates said they were clever bastards and if you got in their way they would make you dead. Maybe the plan was to have me put away for the murder of Coates and then have me killed in prison. I would slip on a bar of soap in the shower, one of the more common causes of death among prisoners in our nation's jails.

Whatever the answers to those questions, it was clear someone wanted to fit me into the frame. But who? The line was growing long enough to require security guards for crowd control.

Following two hours of rough treatment and bad acting, Munich and Martinez let me go. They issued the obligatory warnings—"Don't leave town" and "We'll be watching you, slime bag." These guys were their own cliches. But what do I know, maybe LA cops really talk like that.

I walked out of the police station. I looked at my watch. It was still early. Barely eight o'clock. I was in downtown Los Angeles without a car. I began looking around for a cab.

"Toast!" I heard my name being called. I thought it was Munich changing his mind about cutting me loose. I turned back toward the station. Sherm Bolivia was on the top step.

"Sherm!" I said. "What are you doing here? How did you know I was here?"

"No time to waste, Toast. We're late for services."

"What?"

"The Church of Jesus is in frigging Galilee. My snitch found them operating out of a building in West Hollywood. I tried to call you, but you weren't home."

"How did you know I was here?"

"I drove out to your place to pick up the tapes. I

147

figured you'd be home soon. I got there just as the cops nabbed you. I followed you here. What the hell did you do, anyway? Kill somebody?" Sherm laughed.

"Yeah."

"Huh?" He looked at his watch. "We're wasting time. Services start at eight." Sherm put his hand on my shoulder and pushed me up the street. "My car's parked in the next block.

"I'm not sure I want to tangle with Reverend Swale just now, Sherm."

"Don't go chickenshit on me, Toast. I had to pay my snitch twenty bucks to get this information. I didn't have enough time to get a photographer. We'll have to get pictures later."

"Did I mention these guys carry guns and aren't afraid to use them?"

"You're full of shit, Toast. Here's my car." Sherm unlocked the passenger's door. "Get in."

Chapter 23

Sherm pushed his Chrysler down Sunset in a series of zero-to-sixty accelerations and screeching halts at red lights. That is, when he decided to stop at red lights. He must have burned five gallons of gasoline.

The Jesus is in Galilee Church was located in a small brick building off Olympic Boulevard. It would have taken someone like Sherm's snitch to find it. There were no signs, no lettering on the windows or name on the front door to indicate the brick building was anything other than a brick building.

Sherm led the way. He burst through the front door like they were serving free sirloin steak dinners inside. I was more cautious. We found ourselves in a small enclosed hallway. I looked around. There was nothing on the walls, not even a church bulletin board with announcements of the next rummage sale or the names of the sick who should be paid a visit.

Voices came from beyond the double doors at the end of the hallway. Sherm pushed on. This time he was more careful. He opened the door at the end of the hallway and motioned for me to follow him. I did.

The door opened into a large meeting hall. There were about ten rows of folding chairs facing an elevated stage. An aisle down the middle of the chairs separated the seating into two more or less equal parts. There must have been seventy people sitting in the makeshift pews. On the stage, standing behind a wood podium, was Thurley Swale. He had a book in his hand. It looked like a Bible. He was waving it.

Sherm and I stepped inside the doorway and stood for a few minutes before taking seats in the very last row. It was a big room and our entrance was barely noted.

Reverend Swale was in his shirtsleeves and sweating like a pig. His face was red and his voice loud. He was into one of those lathery, stage-pacing, angry rants that highlight the careers of so many television preachers.

"Twin brothers and sisters in the Lord," he said, walking to the edge of the stage and peering into the faces of his flock.

"The time for truth is drawing closer. I can feel the Last Times are upon us once again. Jesus will sweep down on the people of Christian America and point the finger of accusation at all who failed to believe in Him. The finger of damnation will be thrust upon all those who turned their backs on the Lord and His twin brother and his glorious manifestation to us in the form of the greatest singer the world has ever known.

"He will shame these unbelievers with His songs and smite dead His enemies with a terrible swift sword. Be ye warned all who step on the blue suede shoes of the Lord! Ye of little faith will take a long walk down lonely street from which there will be no return.

"Yes, twin brothers and sisters, the kingdom of Satan is coming to an end. The kingdom of the Lord us upon us. Rock and Roll, forever, twin brothers and sisters, is not the adolescent scream of ignorant youth. No, it is the contemporary coinage of those immortal words from our beloved Lord's Prayer. Rock and roll, forever, means, dear twin brothers and sisters, 'Thy kingdom come, Thy will be done.'

"Elvis as the Lord is among us. Can you feel it? Can you feel the power? Can you feel it? Can you feel that Elvis is standing at the door between heaven and

150

earth waiting for the signal to open that door and reveal Himself as the savior of mankind and lead us into the promised land? Can you feel Him, twin brothers and sisters? Can you see Him standing by that door waiting for a signal? Our signal!"

The congregation, which from the back, looked to be composed of a significant number of huge women in short sleeves that exposed fat, floppy upper arms, began to vocalize the answers to Reverend Swale's provocative questions.

"I see Him!" shrieked several in the folding chairs.

"He is at the door!" someone shouted."

"What is the signal, reverend?" asked several of the flock.

Swale called upon the congregation to close its eyes and pray. As he led them in prayer, a curtain from the rear of the stage parted, uncovering two large portraits sitting on easels. One was of Jesus, the other a gaudy velvet job of Elvis. Between the two paintings was a large wooden cross. At its base was a guitar. A sign in gothic script stood in front of the guitar. It read—"Don't Be Cruel To A Heart That's True."

The services concluded with a singing of some traditional hymns and Elvis tunes. The ritual could have taken place in many churches in America. Only the content and some of the songs were different.

"I'm going to look for the pastor's office," Sherm whispered into my ear. "We can't corner him here." He rose to leave. "You stay here and follow him in case he goes somewhere else. I don't want to lose this baby." Sherm melted into the slowly exiting congregation. I kept my eyes riveted on Swale who was on the stage chatting quietly with two male parishioners who had their backs to me.

After a moment, the two parishioners left him. I didn't take notice as they walked down the aisle toward me. My eyes were on Swale and a female member of the flock he was talking to.

The two parishioners kept coming toward me. I paid them little attention until they stopped in front of me.

"Brother Toast," one of them said. I looked up. It was Twin Brother Osgood. "Reach for the sky," he said. I don't think he meant for me to get closer to God. I didn't see the gun, but I knew he had one. Call it instinct.

I was escorted to a room in the basement. It looked like an office, but it also looked like a store room. There was a desk and a filing cabinet, but there was also a mop, a bucket and a floor buffer in the corner. Twin Brother Osgood and his pal stood at the door. I sat in a folding chair next to the desk. Fifteen minutes later Swale showed up.

"Mr. Toast, how good of you to come."

"The pleasure's all yours."

"Have you brought what we spoke about at your apartment?"

"I still don't know what the hell you are talking about."

"Tsk, tsk, tsk. Have we not treated you with the greatest courtesy?"

"Well, there was that gun you pulled on me."

"Mere ornamentation."

"That puts my mind at ease."

"However, I'm afraid our politeness has its limits. Will you surrender the article? It is most important to my ministry."

"Are you the guys who turned my apartment into an 'as is' store?"

"Please, Mr. Toast. Are you going to cooperate or shall I leave you to the imagination of Twin Brother Osgood?"

"Tell me what it is you're looking for. I'm sure we can make a deal."

"You know very well what we are looking for." Swale's voice approached a shout. "You took it from Coates."

"Did you kill him?"

Thurley Swale straightened up, adjusted the knot in his tie and buttoned his suit jacket. "Very well, then." He turned to Osgood and nodded. He then turned back to me. "You will be speaking in tongues before the night is over." He paused and smiled. "That is, if you have a tongue left. May the Lord have mercy on your soul." Swale turned and left the room.

Twin Brother Osgood rushed me the instant the door closed behind the reverend and slugged me across the face. I fell over backwards. I must have hit my head on something because the only thing I remember was the sound of a choir singing hymns. It could have been coming from upstairs. It could also have been that band of angels coming after me. I hoped it was the former.

Chapter 24

When I came to I heard voices in the distance. One of them sounded like Swale's. I slowly scanned the room from my position on the floor. Except for me the place was empty. I could still hear the voices. That, plus a ringing in my ears from the blow to the head by that gorilla Osgood. I began tracking the voices with my eyes. They were coming from a wall vent about six feet away. Swale and the others must have been upstairs. I couldn't make out what the voices were saying. I could tell there were three men doing the talking, but nothing more substantial than that.

I slowly got to my feet. The blood rushed to my head like it was looking for a place to exit my body. I fought the initial dizziness and made my way for the door. It was locked. I looked around the room for a screwdriver or a letter opener to pry open the lock. I didn't find anything like that, but I found something better. A small window that had been blacked out with paint. It was locked, but opened easily. I climbed through it and in a minute I was on a street behind the church hitching a ride. I wondered what had happened to Sherm Bolivia.

I didn't want to go home. Who knew what was waiting for me there besides a house full of broken furniture and tossed book cases. I called Marty Angelo, but he wasn't in. Neither were a couple of friends who live in West LA. Jan lived nearby in Westwood. I called her. She was in and told me to come right over.

Jan threw her arms around me when she opened the door. "Steve," she said, with a tremble. "You sounded so strange over the phone. Are you all right? Come in, I'll fix you a drink."

When we were inside she noticed the swelling on my jaw. "Steve! Your face. What happened? Were you in an accident? Let me get something for your cheek." She reached out and gingerly touched the side of my face. Tears came to both our eyes.

"Just some cold water and a wash cloth," I said. Jan led me into her living room and sat me down on a sofa while she went for the water and whisky.

The couch was large and soft and pastel. In fact the whole room was pastel. It looked like it had been decorated by a work crew of French impressionists. A fat copy of *Architecture Today* and several issues of *Elegant Apartment* lay on the glass coffee table.

Jan returned carrying a tray. She set it on the coffee table. A bowl and a pastel face towel were to one side, a bottle of Glenfiddich single malt scotch whisky and two glasses to the other. She poured the drinks first. I like a woman who has her priorities straight.

I knocked back the equivalent of two shots in as many gulps. It was smooth and warm. It warmed like those cups of hot cocoa your mother used to give you when you were a kid coming in from playing in the snow.

Jan dipped a corner of the face towel into the water and lightly dabbed my cheek. I took the towel from her and immersed the whole thing into the bowl. I applied it unwrung to my swollen jaw. I leaned over the bowl so as not to drip anything on the coffee table or the thickly piled carpet. I mean friendship only goes so far. Especially with ex-lovers.

I told Jan about the evening services at the Jesus is in Galilee Church. She got that look on her face. The look of pity for a man who has gone around the mental bend and is in need of emergency psychiatric care. I

155

think she would have rather believed I had gotten my lights punched out in a bar fight. It would have made much more sense for the both of us. Whatever she believed, she did her best to humor me. Then she turned argumentative. Surprise.

"Well, why don't you give these people what they want? Is it worth your life to fight them? I mean, it doesn't sound like a case of journalistic ethics here."

"Jan, you haven't been listening. I don't know what they want. They won't tell me what it is. They just assume I have it, but I don't. I'd give it to them if I had it. Believe me."

"How can you not know what it is?"

"I'm telling you, they won't believe me. They just think I'm playing hard to get. Swale babbled something about a sacred religious article. I don't know, maybe they're after one of Elvis' pill bottles."

"Steve. It is all very noble to protect your story and the memory of that man you told me about, but it sounds like your life is in danger. They sound like desperate people. I think you should reconsider." She reached out and took my hand in hers and brought it to her cheek. I pulled back.

"Jan! Whose side are you on? I told you I don't know what the hell it is they want and I don't have it, whatever it is. Period!"

Jan started to tear up. "Steve, I'm just trying to help. I'm frightened for you. You look so, so...."

"Crazy?"

"Steve, please."

"That's what you think, isn't it? That I'm a raving lunatic."

"Stop it!"

"Well, maybe I am. I've worked around the weird for so long, I've finally become demented myself."

"Stop running yourself down. Self-pity doesn't become you. I'm trying to help you think this thing through. Something you have obviously failed to do."

"Ah. Now it comes out. Jan Thomas, bright, intelligent, upward-bounding big city newspaper bureau chief

156

living in luxurious Westwood pulling down a cool 85 grand a year comes to the rescue of her stumblebum ex-lover, the guy who needs written directions to get out of a phone booth. Stay tuned as we see Jan straighten out the miserable gutter journalist yet one more time."

"You have such a chip on your shoulder, Toast. You know that?"

"I had help putting it there."

Jan took my hand in hers again. "Look, Steve. I don't think you're crazy or incompetent. I just want to help."

"Why?"

"Do you really have to ask that question?"

"Yes."

"Look, if we try to think what it is those people want, maybe we can find it and give it to them. That's all they want, right? I mean they won't want to beat you up or anything after they get it, will they?"

I shrugged my shoulders. "I really don't know."

Jan poured me another double shot of Glenfiddich. Two swallows and I was off roving the heather-covered moors of Scotland. I smiled. Jan smiled. My jaw stopped hurting. I remember Jan trying to verbally inventory my worldly possessions before I passed out on the couch.

Chapter 25

When I woke the next morning I was on the sofa and I was alone. My pants were folded on the Aemes chair on the other side of the coffee table. I remembered nothing of the previous night. I was pretty sure I had been a proverbial perfect gentleman if only because I had been a perfectly unconscious gentleman.

I got up and put my pants on. There was a note from Jan lying on the coffee table— "Steve, Don't forget dinner tonight. I know you will make the right career decision. Thanks for last night. Just kidding. Love, Jan."

I had completely forgotten about dinner. I hadn't a sniff of a clue what the right career decision was. And I didn't care for her little joke. It was too much like a sense of humor and that made me uneasy. I folded the note and put it in my pocket.

I met Marty Angelo's sister once about four years ago. I don't remember much about her besides her name and the town where she lived. It was easy to get her number from directory assistance. I looked at my watch. It was a few minutes before nine.

A woman's voice answered the phone at the other end of the line with a strained "hello."

"Is Marty Angelo there?" I asked. "This is his friend, Steve Toast."

The woman laughed cynically. "Mister, Marty Angelo doesn't have any friends, so you can buzz off."

"Wait!" I shouted, before she hung up on me. "Maybe 'friend' is too strong a word. Just tell him it's

Steve Toast. Tell him I have some money for him."

I heard her call into another room. "Hey, Marty, there's a guy on the phone named Toast. Says he has your rent money."

The next voice I heard was Marty's. He sounded scared. "Man, how did you get this number?"

"Marty, I know your sister's last name and I know where she lives. It wasn't that difficult. Why haven't you called?"

"Man, I can't be talking to you anymore for awhile."

"What? Why?"

"The word on the streets is you're hotter than a Bakersfield sidewalk in August."

"What did you find out, Marty?"

"You got the back to that hundred you promised me?"

"Yeah. It's right here in my wallet."

"Tell you what you do. I don't want anyone connecting me with you just now. It might be bad for my health, what with that other little problem hanging over my head at the moment. You take the fifty you owe me and drop it off at the Palm Tree Grill. It's in Hollywood, just off of Sunset. There's a waitress there. A fat broad named Sally. We go around together sometimes. You give the fifty to her. I'll pick it up later this afternoon. Can you get it there before five?"

"Still on the lam, Marty?"

"You're the one who should be lammin' it. From what I hear, the Gobi Desert wouldn't be too safe a place."

"What do you hear?"

"You going to take my fifty to the Palm Tree?"

"Yeah. Give it to a fat broad named Sally."

"You sure? You wouldn't stiff your old pard, would you? I did good work for you, man. Risked my neck for my main man. I need to get paid, you dig?"

"Marty, you will get the money."

"Just looking out for numero uno, Toast. Nothing personal. You'd do the same thing if you were in my

159

shoes."

"Right. Now talk to me, Marty. What did you found out about Coates?"

"Forget him. You've got bigger problems. It's like everybody wants a piece of you, man. What did you do, kill somebody?"

"Yeah. Go on."

Marty laughed nervously. "The cops think you did. And there's some mob types. Word is there is a price on your head. If I was you, Steve, I'd become invisible. Like for about ten years."

"Who would put a price on my head?"

"I don't know for sure, man. It's the kind of question that ends you up as the special meat dish at Mama Gonzoni's Chop House. You know what I mean? But I did hear Abe Switzler is interested in you. I don't know anything more than that."

"What about the Mercury? Did you follow it like I told you? You got a plate for me?"

"I got the plate. You got a pencil? It's OKG 358. I followed it a few blocks, but they spotted me and I had to jackrabbit."

"Did you run a make on the plate?"

"Hey, what do you think a hundred bucks buys these days? Those downtown agencies would have stiffed you for four hundred for what you got off paying only a yard."

"Marty, we both know the going rate is three hundred, not four. Anything else?"

"Yeah. You don't know Marty Angelo and you don't know where to find him."

The phone clicked dead. Marty Angelo sounded like he meant what he said. What spooked him, spooked me, too. It chilled me to think a mafia hit man in the employ of Abe Switzler might be stalking me. And I should be easy enough to find. The cops, the CIA, Reverend Swale and Twin Brother Osgood, the guys in the Mercury. Just look for the guy with a crowd around him.

160

Chapter 26

I fought the temptation to stay at Jan's and ignored the voice inside my head that kept repeating, "Go to LAX, get a flight to the tropics and disappear."

Sometime between my first and second cup of tea I realized I was without a car. In LA that's like going to Disneyland without your wallet. My car was in front of my pad in Venice. Considering all the people sharpening their knives and studying the back of my neck, my apartment was the last place I should go. Why should I make it easy for them? I made a few phone calls and rented a car which I picked up near the UCLA campus.

I was at the DMV before eleven and ran the license plate of the Mercury that had tried to send me onto the off-ramp of life. The DMV kicked back the name Global Entertainment, Inc. It was a company car. The name that went with it was Denton Bozeman. It was a familiar name. One of those names that you see in the newspaper a lot. Like a name of a mogul or near mogul who is a major player in the running of empires in film or real estate.

I looked up Global Entertainment, Inc in the phone book. Its offices were in one of those tower blocks in Century City. I called to find out what Bozeman did at Global Entertainment, Inc.

A very chirpy secretary told me that Denton Bozeman was the CEO for Global Entertainment, Inc.

She said GEI was the corporate parent of a number of well-known subsidiaries that included film studios, record companies, radio stations and a half-dozen cable television stations. The secretary told me Mr. Bozeman would be in his office after two p.m., but that it was impossible to get an appointment.

I drove my rented car over to see Gilbert Talavera at RIO. I was hoping he had been able to dig up something substantial on Coates and the Carter/Elvis/CIA plot. This story assignment had turned into what the literary detectives call a "caper" and this caper needed a major breakthrough.

I walked into the unlocked RIO office. A man was going through the drawers of Gilbert's desk. A man who wasn't Gilbert Talavera. The man looked up at me with a start. "Who are you?" he asked, sharply.

"Steve Toast. And you're...."

"Danny Jones."

"Right. Gilbert's partner."

"Former partner." Jones dropped his eyes and turned away.

"What do you mean, 'former partner'? Did Gilbert quit?"

"Gilbert is dead, man."

"Ohmigod!" My knees began to buckle. I found a chair and sat down.

"Last night. He fell down the outside stairs at his sister's apartment building."

"Fell? Just like that?"

"It was dark. It's an old building and he maybe had too much to drink. His sister said he'd been drinking. He slipped and fell down a whole flight of concrete steps. Snapped his neck like it was a dry twig."

"Are you telling me it was an accident?"

"Who says different? If the nazis or CIA creeps want to get us, they won't make it look like an accident."

"That's not what I heard."

"Then you heard wrong, friend. What we do here is political. Anybody wants to rub us out it will be political and they will want the world to know."

I just sat there in the middle of the RIO office staring blankly at Gilbert's desk. I could almost hear Coates' voice from over my shoulder repeating his words about how the CIA makes people die. But on the other hand, a guy could fall downs his sister's steps, couldn't he? Even a guy like Gilbert Talavera. Couldn't he?

"What did you say your name was, buddy?"

"What?"

"Your name? Toast, isn't it?"

"Yeah."

Danny Jones handed me an envelope. "Here, this is for you. It came in the morning mail. It looks like Gil's handwriting. You can read it over there." He pointed to the computer. I followed the direction of his hand.

I opened the envelope. It contained a fragmented report on computer printout paper:

Coates former CIA employee.

worked in records at Langley

had highest clearance

left 18 mos. ago—official reason: voluntary health retirement (euphemism for mental discharge)

CIA claims C stole classified files when he left (below)

files taken: entire files of OPERATION RAINY NIGHT

RAINY NIGHT: classified, still checking.

nothing on name JAVERT

ran search on Elvis P's known associates. Kicked back two on CIA payroll. Unable to access names. Strange. Will try again.

Hope this helps, Steve. Expect RIO to receive copies of any articles you write or further research turned up. Keep the faith.

Gilbert

ps—have lead how to get names of EP's spooks. Will be in touch.

I read the report again. It raised as many questions as it had answered. What was Operation Rainy

Night? Who were the two CIA agents in Elvis' entourage. Had Coates really been discharged for mental reasons?

However, Gilbert's report had answered one very big question for me. Mental health discharge or not, Coates knew what he was talking about when it came to the CIA. At least the part about it being after him. It wanted its files back.

"Anything good?" Danny Jones' voice broke my concentration.

"Uh, yeah. Gilbert did good work."

"He was the best. He was the one who kept this place running. Now...." He paused and looked around the messy little office. "I don't know. I'm not the researcher Gil was."

"Yeah." I folded the report and put it back into its envelope. I looked at the postmark. I stood up to leave. I took a business card out of my wallet and handed it to Danny Jones. "If you get another envelope for me, you can reach me at this number."

Jones looked at the card and then tossed it onto his desk. "Just between you and me, Toast, I don't think Gilbert will be sending out any more reports."

I held out the envelope for him to see. "This was postmarked two days ago. There might be another one. You never know about the mail."

"Yeah, okay." He picked up my card and put it into his shirt pocket.

I walked to the door. I stopped to take a last look around. Danny Jones was going through some papers on Gilbert's desk. "And Danny," I said.

He looked up. "Yeah?"

"I wouldn't be too quick to accept Gilbert's death as an accident. I don't have to tell you that you're in a business that doesn't believe in accidents."

"Yeah, you don't have to tell me."

"I'd watch my back if I were you. I'm watching mine and I don't like what I see."

"I'll call you if another envelope comes for you."

"Thanks."

Chapter 27

I went to Olvera Street and had a burrito and a sno-cone. I lunched on the bench in front of the fountain where Olvera begins at Macy. I tried to read the sports page, but a gust of wind blew up and turned my newspaper into a kite. Even in hot, dry Los Angeles it is difficult to read a newspaper outside. I have this theory that itinerant bursts of wind freelance through the city looking for people reading newspapers and swoop down on them. Sort of like high-flying hawks looking for lunch.

I balled up the newspaper and threw it away. Another gust of wind kicked up some dirt and blew it toward me. The front page of a rival tabloid came to rest at my feet. I glanced down at the headline— "Battery Cables Jumpstart Dead Man's Heart."

I got up and walked over to Union Station for a cup of tea and a piece of pie just to kill some time and get out of the wind.

At fifteen minutes past two I was parking my rented car inside a building in Century City. Global Investments, Inc has a wing of suites on the twenty-second floor of one of those smoked glass jobs that have remade the Southland skyline. The reception area had dark, thick carpeting, rich and conservative furniture and the wallpaper was most sensible.

I walked up to the receptionist and told her I wanted to see Denton Bozeman. I told her I didn't have an appointment.

"No," she said. "You can't see Mr. Bozeman. He is a very busy man and you must have an appointment. That is the only way you can possibly see him."

She wasn't the one I had talked to earlier. This one looked like she strongly identified with the corporation and was as loyal to her boss as a German shepherd. If her arms hadn't been covered with the sleeves of a plum-colored blouse, I would bet one of them would have sported a tattoo that read—"Born To Say No."

"My name is my appointment. Steve Toast."

"Please leave, sir. I will call security if you don't. Believe me, I will."

"Why don't you call your Mr. Bozeman? Tell him Toast of the *COMET* is here. He will want to see me."

"You are just wasting your time and mine. Now be a good boy and go back to Venice, or wherever it is you come from." She cracked a brittle smile. It was the sort of smile the rich and self-important wear when addressing people who aren't. It was all the more pathetic because the receptionist was not rich and her self-importance came from vicariously living the lives of the people she worked for.

I leaned over her desk and reached for the phone on her console. She shrieked and lunged for the phone to prevent me from touching her instrument. I let her win.

"Good," I said. "Now pick it up and call Mr. Bozeman like the good little corporate drone you are. You'll see, your boss will want to see me. I'm not going back to the institution until you call him."

"The what?" She looked at me like, yes, maybe he is an escapee from a mental ward. She slowly picked up the phone and reached out her finger to push one of the buttons on the console.

"Call security and I'll bite your neck." Her finger went straight to the button marked "CEO".

"Mr. Bozeman," she said, apologetically. "I'm very sorry to bother you, sir, but there is a man out here who

166

insists on seeing you.... No, sir, I don't think he is an actor.... I did tell him he would have to make an appointment, but he is quite threatening.... I don't think I can, sir.... He said you would want to meet him... He said his name is Toast.... That's what he said. Toast from the.... Yes, sir. I will send him in."

She put the phone down and looked at me like I was a normal person. "Mr. Bozeman will see you now, sir." She smiled like we were old friends. She stood up and led me to the door directly behind her. "Have a pleasant day, Mr. Toast." I rolled my eyes and walked past her into Denton Bozeman's office.

Bozeman was standing at parade rest in front of the wall-sized window looking out at the smog. He turned when I got halfway across the room. The two-inch pile carpeting slowed me down.

"Sit down, Mr. Toast?" I sat down in a chair made of rich brown leather, the kind Ricardo Montalban used to talk about in those car commercials on TV. "What can I do for you?"

"You can start by not trying to have me killed."

"I beg your pardon." Bozeman was tall, lean and fifty-five. His suit was as rich and conservative as the furniture. He sat down in a chair across from me and crossed his legs. He seemed no more concerned than if I had come to tell him his tires needed rotating.

"Let me put it this way, Mr. Bozeman. Big, late model Mercury. Four-door. Silver grey. License number OKG 358. Does any of that ring a bell?"

"It could be one of our company cars. I would have to check the license plate against our fleet manifest to be sure."

"Let me save you the time. I checked it with DMV and surprise, it is registered to you."

"We have some ten or twelve automobiles. I don't see your point."

"My point is, whoever has been driving that car the past few days has tried to kill me. Someone in that car fired a shot at me in Venice. It has been following me for the last four days. I want some answers, Bozeman."

167

"I think you are jumping to conclusions, Mr. Toast. No one in my employ has made an attempt on your life. I will admit that I have had you followed."

"Aha! Why?"

"Purely professional reasons, I assure you."

"Oh?"

"Yes. I am glad you came here, Mr. Toast. My staff has been trying to contact you for two days to set up a meeting with you. You are a very elusive man, you know that?"

"Yeah. They call me 'Butter' at the office."

"Butter Toast. Very amusing." Bozeman smiled, but not very much.

"So, what did you want to see me about? I'm a reporter for the *National COMET*. You have a sheep that gave birth to a human baby?"

"I think you know what this is about?"

"Why does everyone assume I know what's going on? Don't overestimate my intelligence. It will get both of us into trouble."

"It has to do with your association with a man named Coates."

"Former association. He's dead, but I'm not telling you anything new, am I?"

"I will try to ignore your sarcasm."

"Everyone does."

"We know you were meeting with him. We have some tapes of an interview you did with him."

"So, you're the guys who turned my place into shredded wheat. It figures."

"Do you know anything about Global Entertainment, Mr. Toast?"

"You are something like the Standard Oil of the entertainment industry."

"Not quite, but close." Bozeman stood up and went to a wooden globe that was resting on a floorstand next to his glass-topped desk. I thought he was going to point out his company's vast holdings, but instead, he lifted the top of the globe and pulled out a bottle of whisky. He poured himself a drink into a glass he

168

picked from the shelf of a fake bookcase that opened into a cupboard. He took his drink and sat on the edge of his desk very casual-like.

"GEI owns approximately 15% of the combined television, radio and motion picture industry in the United States and nearly 10% of the recording business. We own more than forty companies outright and controlling interest in another seventy-five. We are ranked thirteenth on the Fortune 500, but could easily be higher in the near future."

"So, business is great. Glad to hear it."

"Not exactly. GEI has backed some high risk projects during the last two years that have become financial Titanics. We invested thirty million into a mini-series on the life of Calvin Coolidge"

"Never heard of it."

"Exactly. It was a disaster. Tony Danza was cast for the lead. We should have seen that one coming."

"I see what you mean?"

"And we backed the reunion tour of the Chocolate Wristwatch."

"The who?"

"I wish it had been the Who. Heads started rolling when the grosses from the tour and record sales began trickling in. They never did more than trickle."

"So, business is not so great."

"Currently we are fighting a leveraged buyout mounted by the Germans."

"Times are tough all over. What's this got to do with Yours Truly?"

"One of the brighter spots in the GEI stables is our recording companies. Despite the loss with the Chocolate Wristwatch we have signed a number of contemporary stars. Mostly country and western, but we have a classical label and a new jazz imprint. We have also purchased the rights to songs of performers no longer living. It is a very steady market. All we have to do is keep the records in print and make small royalty payments to the estates. We are at a point where we could make a significant breakthrough in the record business. With the projects we currently have under contract we could add as many as seven points to our share of the market. That's close to double what we have now. Not only that, but these projects could turn around the slide GEI has been experiencing. If we have a big winner we are back in the ball game."

"And I suppose you have one, right?"

"I have personally brokered the deal that got GEI the rights to more than one hundred Elvis Presley records. We have been re-releasing them for about four years. Our market share has been rising about one-half point a year, largely due to the revenue brought in by Elvis recordings. Then, a year ago, a man came to me with a proposal so fantastic that I originally had him thrown out of my office."

I tilted my head toward the door and the receptionist beyond. "I know the feeling."

"But subsequently, I was brought around to his position. I wasn't won easily. Documentary evidence, personal contacts and the steady rise of record sales of a man I thought had been dead for more than ten years."

"Thought had been dead?"

"Yes, thought! I became persuaded that Elvis Presley is alive. I know it sounds crazy, but I saw the nail wounds in the hands, so to speak. The proof was overwhelming. So I bought twelve new songs Presley has recorded since 1977. I tell you, the feeling around here was not unanimous. I went to the wall on this."

"I bet you did. I just hope it was a rubber one."

"The purchase of the master came relatively cheap. But GEI has sunk a fortune it no longer has into a publicity campaign that is set for launching in less than six weeks. We have pressed eight million copies, both LP and CD. The projected net revenues are $48.2 million. That is corporate turnaround revenue, Mr. Toast. It's career-making revenue for me if the project is a success."

"And you're staking all this on the very dubious notion that Elvis Presley is alive and well and some-

170

where recording new tunes."

"Quite frankly, I don't personally give a rat's ass whether the man is alive or dead. What's important is that there are thirty million Elvis fans out there who do. Thirty million people who will buy a ten dollar album of new songs recorded by the King of Rock and Roll. The eight million is just the first pressing. I'm confident we can sell thirty million of the suckers. That's $48.2 million multiplied by four."

"Two hundred million dollars from a record that could have been recorded by anybody? No wonder GEI is going down the drain."

"Hold on! I didn't get where I am by falling for grifters and con men. And God knows the entertainment industry is lousy with them. We had the voice of the master recording submitted to rigorous and thorough analysis by four different voice print experts. They all came back with positive reports. It's Elvis' voice, not an imitator or a patch job. The most skeptical of the four experts was 87% convinced. The other three were above 95%. We have printed their affidavits on the album cover."

"Gee, that would convince me."

"What we have is the greatest event in the recording business since Edison invented the gramophone. When *ELVIS: Live Again After All These Years* hits the stores there will be a buying frenzy never before witnessed in this country."

"Good luck."

"There is one problem."

"Why did I think there was?"

"You see, in order for this album to sell, we have to be able to convince people that there is a strong possibility that Elvis is alive. Otherwise we've got an expensive hoax on our hands and no one will buy the record. GEI will be out ten million dollars."

"And Denton Bozeman will be in the supper line at St. Paul's Mission."

"So, you see we can't afford any negative publicity that will sabotage the album launch. The word I have

171

received is that you have been in contact with this man Coates and are preparing to run a series of articles about the death of Elvis Presley at the hands of the CIA."

"And you'd rather I not write anything like that."

"You can see what it would do to the album sales."

"What if it's the truth? What if the CIA did kill Elvis?"

"Truth?" Denton Bozeman laughed a loud, cynical laugh. "Forgive me, but what the hell do you care about the truth? You work for a newspaper that routinely runs banner headlines about television programs beamed from Mars and mothers who sell their children to buy cat food."

"You've got me there, but this is different. I think there is something going on here. I want to find out what it is."

"Would, say, $25,000 dampen your curiosity?"

"You trying to buy me off?"

"Just a small cost in our publicity budget. All good publicity campaigns try to neutralize negative publicity. The price is worth is to us."

"And if I say no?"

"I can sweeten the pot up to a point. I'm counting on you being a reasonable man, Mr. Toast."

"Well, I am reasonable about a lot of things. I wear sensible shoes and don't date above my class. And $25,000 sounds fine to me."

Denton Bozeman smiled and walked to the fake bookcase. He took down another glass and walked over to the globe. He picked up the bottle of whisky.

"But," I said, before he began pouring, "I have a personal investment in this story. I would like to see it through to the end."

Bozeman returned the bottle of whisky to the globe unpoured. He closed the lid and walked back to his desk. He pressed a button on his phone console.

"That is a very unwise choice, Mr. Toast."

"I can live with it."

"That may not be as easy as you think. I strongly

172

urge you to reconsider. I'll make it $50,000." The cool detachment was gone from Denton Bozeman's voice. He sounded worried, maybe even a bit frightened. It was a cinch, however, his worry and fear had nothing to do with my well-being.

I looked him directly in the face. "You've got more than your job on the line with this Elvis record, don't you?"

"I don't know what you are talking about."

"I mean you stand to lose more than your numbered parking space and your membership in the Athletic Club."

"You are the one we are talking about, not me."

"You've got mafia money sunk into this album, haven't you? If it flops, you're wearing cement cycling shorts at the bottom of a Beverly Hills swimming pool."

"What on earth gave you that absurd idea?"

"Abe Switzler has put a price on my head."

"I'm not familiar with the name."

"Sure you are. Abe Switzler is the mafia's loan officer for Southern California. Easy credit terms, but the penalties for nonpayment you don't want to hear about. The way I figure it, Switzler is probably gunning for me for the same reason you are. However, if I somehow manage to slip through his fingers and print my stories, it's you who'll be number one on his hit parade."

"This is your last chance, Toast."

"What? You going to call in some of your mobster business partners to take me for a ride?" I laughed once through my nose. "This isn't one of your TV shows."

Bozeman shook his head and pressed a button on his phone console. A side door to his office opened. A man as big as the Santa Monica Pier walked in.

Bozeman pointed to me. "Take him for a ride. You know where."

173

Chapter 28

Okay, so I was wrong. What I wanted to know was what was I doing in the back seat of a Mercury with a gun in my ribs instead of standing in line at my bank waiting to deposit $50,000 into my account? Talk about not knowing how to make the right career decisions.

I guess I didn't think a record company would kill people. How foolish. I mean, don't the rumors still persist that it was a record company that was responsible for the airplane crash that killed Otis Redding? And if there is any truth in that, what about Buddy Holly and Richie Valens and Patsy Cline? Isn't it strange that only recording artists die in plane crashes? Jim Croce, the Big Bopper, Rick Nelson. Don't tell me movie stars and television personalities don't fly. Maybe I was being taken to an airport instead of a deserted canyon. Then again, maybe not.

It was some small comfort to know that I had finally figured out what was going on. In another forty minutes I could share my information with eternity.

So, it was an entertainment industry mogul and a mafia banker protecting their mutual investment that led to Coates' death and maybe the death of Gilbert Talavera as well. No wonder Marty Angelo was having a hysterical episode when I talked to him. It seemed like people I talked to were marked for death. Was Bob Watts next? Or Jan? Were they scheduled to die from

174

'natural causes', too? Was this the new mafia at work? What happened to gangland killings that we have all come to know over the years?

All this to perpetuate the belief, the fanatic hope, that the King of Rock and Roll is still alive. I guess the potential sale of $200 million worth of record albums made it all worth it for them. Corporate entertainment and organized crime. Partners in greed and bad judgement. Somehow it all made sense to me. Perfect sense.

The car sped west on the Santa Monica Freeway to the Coast Highway. There it turned north and turned off onto Topanga Canyon and began ascending the windy road that goes through the Santa Monica Mountains.

There was still a lot that I couldn't answer. Like the bottom line truth to Coates' theories about the CIA. And Reverend Swale's real motive behind his search for the holy Elvis artifact. Was he just another religious nut or was he connected with all the others? If so, what was the connection? Who were the others? If I had had the time I could have probably figured it all out, but I had other things on my mind at the moment. Like dealing with the guys who were taking me for a ride. Big problem was I had no idea how to deal with guys like them who take guys like me for rides.

It wasn't summer yet, so the mountains were green and soft. I could pick out the colors of wildflowers as the big Mercury climbed into the mountains, no doubt heading for some remote area to turn me into compost. I began to shiver noticeably.

I tried to make conversation with the Santa Monica Pier. "You don't have to kill me, you know," I said, getting right to the point.

"Shut up!"

"No, really. I've reconsidered Mr. Bozeman's offer. I'll take his money and leave the country if he wants."

"Shut up!"

"You don't think I went up to Bozeman's office alone, do you? You think I'm that stupid? I called the cops. They've been tailing us ever since we left Century

175

City. Give up now and I will testify you were only acting under orders. Seriously."

"Shut up!" His arm shot out and jabbed me below the ribs. I saw stars for a minute. It was his way of ending the conversation.

A few minutes later the Santa Monica Pier leaned forward and tapped the driver on the shoulder. "This is it," he said. He punched me in the arm. "End of the line, for you, Gabby." He reached across me and opened the door. "Get out!" I got out.

"I suppose I just walk toward the bushes and you shoot me in the back," I said. My heart was pounding like the kettle drums in a Wagner opera. My legs felt like spaghetti. Cooked spaghetti. The Santa Monica Pier smiled obscenely and motioned with his gun for me to start walking. When I didn't move fast enough for him he gave me a hard shove in the back. I tripped over a rock and went sprawling to the ground.

"Get up!" he growled.

I rolled over and saw his gun pointing at my head. I felt like fainting. I wanted to faint. I didn't want to be conscious at my own execution. I held my breath. I thought maybe, if I was lucky, I would black out.

"I said get up, fuck face!" I was beginning to feel light-headed. I closed my eyes and very slowly began to get up. I thought I heard a car engine followed by the squeal of brakes and tires sliding on gravel. Then I heard doors opening and people shouting. I chanced one eye.

I saw two men pointing guns from behind the open doors of a car that was not the big, grey Mercury. I wasn't hallucinating. I started breathing again.

"Let him go!" shouted one of the gun men. It was a request with which I was in total sympathy. However, I was the only one. He was answered with a volley of shots coming from the guns of the Santa Monica Pier and the driver of the Mercury. They were a little slow on the draw. A short, loud exchange of gunfire left my abductors lying in the dirt with bullet holes in their vital places.

The two gun men from the second car rushed me. I wanted to thank them for saving my life. I got to my feet and stuck out a grateful hand. It was ignored by both of them. One of the ignorers was Twin Brother Osgood. He grabbed me by the back of the collar and frog marched me to his car and stuffed me into the back seat. The car squealed away kicking up a wheelbarrow full of dirt and stones.

Chapter 29

Instead of going back to the Jesus is in Galilee Church in west Hollywood, the car turned north when it got to Westwood and drove past the UCLA campus and into the hills of Bel Air.

Bel Air is another snooty LA neighborhood. The houses have burglar alarm systems that cost more than most average people pay for their houses. There are no sidewalks in Bel Air. If you want to go for a walk you jump in your Mercedes. People on foot in Bel Air are considered prowlers and the police are called.

The car turned off Beverly Glen. A few streets later it rolled into a driveway lined with exotic bushes from foreign countries. The house looked like a French chateau as it might have been designed by an architect who was getting paid by the brick. At a dollar a brick, the place must have cost three million bucks. And that is excluding the Italian marble fountain in the front yard.

Twin Brother Osgood opened the car door and escorted me into the house. The place looked like the owner was in competition with the Getty Museum. A front room that opened off the foyer was chock full of oil paintings, marble and bronze statues and very French furniture, probably eighteenth century. Flemish tapestries lined the foyer.

I was taken into a library that had more leather

than an S & M bar. The chairs were leather and so were the covers of the antique books. Even the drapes looked leather, but I doubt if they were. It could have been the lighting. It was soft and golden. I felt like I had stepped into a Rembrandt painting.

"Mr. Toast," said the man sitting behind the large, dark wood desk. "So good of you to come on such short notice."

"I was in the process of being murdered. I was glad to do it."

He turned to the man seated in the leather recliner to his right. "I believe you know Reverend Swale."

I looked at Swale. He smiled ever so slightly while nodding his head. "Yeah," I said. "We go to the same church."

"Reverend Swale informs me you possess something we would very much like to have."

"We? You guys working together? Somehow you don't look like the Elvis is Alive in Galilee type."

"Jesus is in Galilee," Twin Brother Osgood snorted from his standing station by the door.

The man behind the desk continued. "I share Reverend Swale's interest in the object in question. My interest, however, is more secular." His manner was as civil as a Riverside County orange.

"You know," I said, mustering as much sincerity as a person in my position could muster, "this may come as a big surprise to you and maybe even a greater disappointment, but I don't know what the bloody hell you guys are talking about." My voice was running up the decibel meter and was approaching a desperate shout. "What object in question? Will somebody please tell me? I'd really like to know."

"Mr. Toast," tsked the man behind the desk. "I am prepared to pay a price for the recovery of the object. A very handsome price."

"I'll take it! I'll take it! Just tell me what the hell it is you want!"

The man looked at Swale. "He knows," Swale said. "He was a confidant of Coates."

179

"The collector you spoke of?" the man behind the desk asked, rhetorically.

"The collector and satanic agent of Paul the defiler of the word of the Lord."

"Spare me the sermon, reverend. Does this man know what we want or not? You told me he has the object."

"I said he has it or knows where it is."

"Object!" I interrupted. "What bloody, stinking object?"

A silence clanked down over the room like the bars to maximum stir. Twin Brother Osgood turned red in the face. Thurley Swale narrowed his eyes and squinted two thousand years of hate at me. The man behind the desk had a look quilted on his face that said "time is money," like he was wasting too much of the former and not earning enough of the latter.

"Perhaps, then," he said, "I should tell you precisely what it is I, we want."

"You are a tribute to your class, sir," I said with only the hint of sarcasm.

"I am a collector, Mr. Toast. Perhaps you saw some of my Rodins and canvases in the atrium as you came in today."

"Hard to miss, actually."

"I don't know, call it an obsession of a man who has everything or perhaps an expensive hobby or even a disease of the soul if you like, but I must possess things that other people cannot. That is the nature of a collector. A true collector. To own things rare and exotic. A Shakespeare first folio, a Louis XV armoire, a four hundred year-old Yoruba mask, a Mickey Mantle rookie baseball card. It does not matter. It is the possession of the thing that counts. That and the hunt to possess it. And if the object possessed is so rare that there is only one of them in existence, then, Mr. Toast, that is the ultimate reward of collecting. The supreme satisfaction.

"I possess things, Mr. Toast. One of a kind things. I have more than one hundred original paintings and drawings by the great masters spanning four centuries.

I have the largest collection of Miros in America. But I am not only an art collector. I have other collections that are equally valuable to me. I have a pre-1900 collection of advertising art. Signs, posters, buttons and the like. I have the earliest known box of Smith Brothers cough drops in existence. It is valued at $28,000. I also have the original Howdy Doody marionette and a sizable collection of the finest fountain pens ever made. I have three Tucker automobiles. Do you know how many Tuckers there are in existence, Mr. Toast?" I shook my head no. The man behind the desk didn't tell me. It was one of those rhetorical questions.

"One of my newer interests, one that has become a passion with me, is my Elvis Presley collection. I have first pressings of most of his albums, major props from *Viva Las Vegas* and *Blue Hawaii*, letters Elvis wrote when he was in the army in Germany and many other collectibles too numerous to mention."

The man behind the desk stopped and smiled as if he were expecting some kind of approval from me for all the things he owned. He was scary. I was waiting for him to break into a maniacal Peter Lorre laugh and for me to go screaming up a wall. Neither one of us did either.

"What I am hungering to possess," he continued, pausing for a moment to look at Swale and then amend his comment, "What we want very badly is Elvis Presley's last jumpsuit."

"Last jumpsuit?" I muttered under my breath, trying not to betray my astonishment.

"It was the last costume Elvis wore in public performance," Swale added, as if to say that it was well worth kidnapping and beating me, not to mention the numberless murders of people who had inconvenienced them in their search for it.

"It was a new and more elaborate garment than any of the others he had previously worn," said the man behind the desk. "It had a larger, more expensive rhinestone and diamond trim."

"Don't forget the stain," Swale added.

181

"Reverend Swale and his followers believe there is a sweat stain on the garment that has a certain religious significance."

"It is a perfect outline of the face of the Virgin," Swale said. "It is the sign that Elvis is the Lord and is planning to return to save mankind."

"It was the costume Elvis wore to his last concert," continued the man behind the desk. "It disappeared shortly after August 16, 1977. I have been trying to locate it for nearly five years. I had heard that it was destroyed in a fire at the home of a Nashville collector in 1983. Then it resurfaced two years later in a safety deposit vault in Washington D.C. where it was among the items stolen in one of the biggest bank robberies of modern times. I lost track of it until it turned up here in Los Angeles in the possession of your Mr. Coates."

"What's this jumpsuit worth?" I asked.

"In dollars, oh, I'd say probably not more than 85-to-100,000. But it is not its monetary value that interests me."

"It's the hunt, right?"

The man behind the desk smiled at me. He liked a good listener. "And, of course, the rarity of the garment. To a serious Elvis collector like myself, this is like the Holy Grail." He paused and looked at Swale. "So, now you know what we want and why we want it. Are you prepared to help us, Mr. Toast?"

I cleared my throat and looked at a painting on the library wall. It looked like a Lautrec and I was convinced it was no copy. "I don't have this jumpsuit, if that's what you mean by help. I don't know where it is, either. Honest."

Swale pounded his fist into the arm of his chair. "I told you he wouldn't cooperate! He is only interested in writing the lies and slanders of that pathetic spreader of Paulist poison."

The man behind the desk waved his hand for Swale to stop. "The religious aspect of this matter does not concern me." He looked at me. " I am only interested in obtaining the last jumpsuit Elvis Presley ever

182

wore. If you are standing by some kind of journalistic ethic, Mr. Toast, I would advise you to abandon it before it is too late. Such false heroism can only put you at risk. Rather grave risk. I will tell you quite frankly that I am a man who knows what he wants. More importantly, I am a man who gets what he wants. I will get the jumpsuit whether I pay you or have you erased from the face of the earth. It is your choice, Mr. Toast." He looked at his watch. "You don't have much time,"

I ran my hand over the back of my neck. It was wet and cold and on the chopping block. "Tell you what," I said. "Why don't I just give you what you want and we can shake hands and part friends. This thing has turned into a giant headache for me and I'd just as soon get rid of it."

"That is very generous of you, Mr. Toast, but I pay full and fair prices for my purchases. I will pay you $25,000 for the jumpsuit." The man behind the desk smiled with satisfaction. "Splendid! Now, when can we collect the garment? Might I suggest we do it immediately?"

Swale stood up and moved behind his chair. "Twin Brother Osgood and I will go get it."

"Ah," I said. "There's a slight problem, gentlemen."

"Problem?" the man behind the desk repeated, as if I had just told him to go to hell in a foreign language.

"I don't actually have it in my possession." I was dog paddling in deep water. I didn't have Elvis Presley's jumpsuit and probably wouldn't have recognized it if I were wearing it. But they thought I had it and weren't going to let me out of Chateau Creepy unless I delivered the goods. It gave me a little time to come up with something to deal my way out of trouble.

"Where is it?" Swale demanded. He turned to his patron. "I think he's playing with us. It's Satan's way. This man represents a malignant growth on the body of our work. We must act swiftly to cut it out before it spreads and puts our mission at further risk. The Lord said, I bring you a sword...."

"Whoa!" I shouted. "I know where it is. I can take

183

you to it."

"If what you say is true," said the man behind the desk, "we will send someone to get it. You will remain here with us."

"Uh, it's not quite that simple."

"I trust you can explain that."

Swale was growing more agitated by the minute. "I think we should turn this serpent's agent of Paul and Colonel Parker over to Twin Brother Osgood."

"Wait! Wait!" I protested. "No need for that. We can work this thing out."

"It would be preferable," said the man behind the desk.

"Coates kept a locker," I said, paddling toward an imaginary shore. "Yeah. Coates told me about it before you guys croaked him." I looked at Swale.

"We have not croaked anyone, as you put it. Yet!"

"Right. Well, there is this locker at Union Station."

"We don't need you for that," Swale cut in. "We just need the locker number and the key."

"There is no key. Coates didn't want a key. He felt it would be too easy for it to fall into the wrong hands, no offense intended."

"How is one to gain access to the locker?" asked the man behind the desk.

"Coates told me that when the time came, I would go to the baggage room at Union Station and present my driver's license to a man who works there named Jackson. If Jackson is satisfied with my identity he will give me the key to the locker.

Swale shook his head. "Sounds like a trick. I can smell the handiwork of the wily Colonel Parker himself."

"No! Honest. If you knew Coates, you would know this is the way he operated."

Swale was still unconvinced. "Why didn't you tell me this the first time we met?"

"I didn't know what you wanted."

"You knew!"

"Honest. This is the first time I've heard about any

184

jumpsuit."

"What? What did you think was in Coates' locker? A change of underwear?

Swale was persistent. I couldn't hold him off much longer. He was asking all the right questions. They weren't too hot to handle for someone who had the right moves. I had spent my professional life asking questions of professional smoke-throwers and dodge artists. Now, the tables had been turned and I was being called upon to throw a big fog ball past Swale and the others. I reached back into the old gray stuff one more time.

"Coates never really told me what was in the locker. He just said it was valuable. He led me to believe it had something to do with the CIA. You guys aren't CIA, are you?"

Swale looked at me like I had called him a Catholic. The man behind the desk examined his manicure waiting for me to go on.

"Then how do you know the garment is in the locker?" Swale asked. That was the $64 question, wasn't it? It was now or never. It was Drysdale and Hershiser time. Time to throw your best pitch and shut out the other guys.

"To tell you the honest truth, I don't know for sure. I didn't know Coates was an Elvis collector until I went to his house the night he was killed. I didn't put it all together until yesterday. If there is a last Elvis Presley jumpsuit in this world and Coates had it, I'd bet my life it is in that locker at Union Station."

"You just did!" said Swale.

I didn't like his use of the past tense. I looked at the man behind the desk. There was a certain twinkle in his eye. A nervousness, maybe. A mania. The hunt was on again and he could smell the game.

"Gentlemen," he said, looking around the room. "It's worth a try. Let's go do it." He smiled at Swale. Swale smiled back. I didn't like that, either.

Chapter 30

I was put into the back seat of yet another large sedan. I figured as long as I was in the back seat of these gas hogs I was okay. Being taken for a ride is not what gets people dead. It's what happens at the end of those rides.

I also figured I was buying myself some time. Every minute was another moment in which something might happen to pull me out of the briar patch. Swale and the man behind the desk didn't come right out and say it, but I knew what waited for me at the end of the ride. I'm no dope. I've watched all the reruns of the *Rockford Files*. When Rockford was in a tight spot and would make a deal with the bad guys for his life, the bad guys always welshed and tried to kill him. The way I looked at it I was in a similar situation. It didn't matter whether I delivered the jumpsuit or not. They weren't going to let me walk away. I knew it and they knew it. I was hoping that they didn't know I knew it.

Driving in to Union Station, I put it all together. I really had it figured out this time. Swale and the rich collector had killed Coates because he wouldn't part with the jumpsuit. Swale had a second and more important motive. For his own religious reasons he didn't like Coates spreading stories that Elvis was dead. That gave him the same motive as Bozeman and Abe Switzler. They could have all been working together on this, but that little shoot-out in Topanga Canyon told me they probably weren't.

Yet, there were still a few unanswered questions. Like why would Swale and the collector want to kill Gilbert Talavera? Unless they wanted more than the jumpsuit and were connected with the CIA. I refused to consider that Gilbert's death was an accident, but removing him from the equation made the Swale-collector scenario work much better.

I couldn't tie everything with a nice yellow bow because there were one or two other things on my mind that seemed at least equally as important. Number one was to come up with something between Bel Air and Union Station that would save my bacon. There was nobody named Jackson in the baggage room at the station and there certainly was no key to any locker that contained any Shroud of Memphis with or without sweat stains that looked like any Virgin. And like I said, even if there were, the problem for me remained the same.

The big sedan lumbered east along Sunset Boulevard. Swale and Twin Brother Osgood were sitting on either side of me in the back seat. Another church faithful was behind the wheel. The man behind the desk stayed behind at his chateau. Although I don't think Swale bought my story, I was given the benefit of the doubt. No handcuffs, guns in the ribs or angry snorts from Twin Brother Osgood. He sat meekly humming hymns to himself while he looked out the window.

Sunset Boulevard is wide all the way into downtown. There are lots of stoplights, but the traffic was moving at a fairly good clip. Sunset runs behind UCLA, past Holmby Hills Golf Course and the better homes in Beverly Hills. Then it enters Hollywood and becomes "The Strip". Funny, the things you think about when in life-threatening situations. Life-ending situations. All I could think about as we entered Hollywood was William Holden lying face down in Gloria Swanson's swimming pool in the movie *Sunset Boulevard*. I thought about how Holden was already dead, but still

187

was the narrator of the story. A dead man telling a tale. I felt a lot like Holden. Weird. Hollywood does that to people.

The car slowed down as it approached downtown Hollywood and it wasn't to take in the sights. Sunset was choked with people and cars. It was near gridlock. I looked out the window. We were nearing the Chinese theatre. I thought there must be another ceremony immortalizing yet another star's footprints in concrete. From the size of the crowd it had to be somebody big. Like maybe Ed McMahon or Vanna White.

Swale grew impatient. He leaned forward to say something to the driver. He rose partway from the back seat. Someone or something must have jumped out in front of the car. The driver slammed on the brakes and Swale went sprawling over the front seat. It was a moment I had been hoping for. I turned and butted my head into his side. He went crashing into the door.

"Osgood!" he wailed.

I reached across him and pulled the door handle. I felt the steel barrel of Osgood's gun lightly graze the back of my head in a near-miss swing as I propelled myself out the door entangled with Swale.

We hit the pavement and rolled to the curb. I gave Swale a short chop to the jaw to disengage myself from him. I rolled onto the sidewalk where I knocked down two blondes wearing spandex shorts and bikini tops. Some other people stumbled over us. All I could see was knees and shoes.

At that moment the screaming and shouting started. I don't know if any punches were thrown, but there was a lot of shoving. It took all the strength I had just to get to my knees. I crawled into the doorway of a a skateboard shop. I had footprints all over my body.

I got to my feet and briefly surveyed the situation. I had lost Swale, but in the next instant I was pinned by a solid wall of people all shouting and shoving in an attempt to break free from the grip of the mob. It felt like one of those rock concerts where the crowd panics and a hundred people get crushed to death. But this

188

was LA, the land of options. No need for anyone to get trampled to death, unless, of course, that was what the mob wanted.

For a brief moment that is exactly what I thought it wanted. It pressed helpless people at the edge of the throng up against the glass windows and doors of the shops. I was still trapped in the doorway of the skateboard shop like a fly between storm windows. I couldn't open the door to get in or push back the surging hundreds. I was pressed against the door. I could see the people inside the store, their faces and bodies frozen with horror as they watched our distorted faces being pressed against the glass.

Then, like low tide, the crowd inexplicably receded. It was done quietly and uniformly and left great hunks of space to breathe and room to feel alive. The look of relief was apparent in every face. Another Hollywood star event had passed into history without any fatalities.

Chapter 31

By the time I worked my way loose from the crowd I was several blocks away. I ducked into a cafe for a cup of tea. I sat at the counter. The waitress came over with a pot of coffee and began filling my cup without asking. I started to protest, but stopped. Her eyes were red and raw and her hand was unsteady as she poured.

"Having a rough day?" I asked.

"Yeah, pretty," she sniffed. "We had a shooting right outside less than two hours ago."

"Really? That's awful. Did you see it?"

"I knew the guy they killed."

I poured sugar and milk into the coffee to help kill the taste. "That makes it even worse. Sorry to hear that. Did you know him well?"

"He wasn't much. Kind of a creep, really. But Marty was okay sometimes. We had a few laughs together."

"Marty?" I swallowed more coffee in the gulp that I took than I had drunk in six months.

"He was a grifter and con artist, sure. And he would stiff me with the check when we went out to dinner every chance he could. But that don't mean someone has to go and kill him, does it?"

"Marty who?"

"I saw it right through the window. A big car pulled up and rolled down its window. A guy pointed a gun at

Marty and just shot him. It all happened so fast." The waitress fought back a tear.

"Marty Angelo? Are you talking about Marty Angelo?"

"Yeah. Did you know him?"

"They killed Marty?"

"In cold blood."

"Did you see who did it? Was it a big grey Mercury?"

"I just saw Marty laying there on the sidewalk in all that blood. It was awful. Somebody must have really hated Marty to do that to him."

The waitress continued talking to me, but I wasn't listening. I was making a mental list of the deaths of people connected to Coates and me. Could I now add Marty Angelo to the list? There were a lot of people who wouldn't have minded seeing Marty planted in a pine box, but I don't think they would go to the extreme of doing it themselves. There was his latest con that had gone sour. Maybe it was more serious than I thought. Marty thought it was serious enough to go into hiding. It must have been the marks who killed Marty. I kept telling myself that until I nearly became convinced.

"More coffee, mister?" the waitress said.

"What?"

"Coffee. You want some more."

"No."

I got up from the stool and peeled off two twenties and a ten from my wallet and slid them under the coffee cup. The waitress saw me do it and her eyes went into orbit.

"Are you nuts, mister? A fifty dollar tip?"

"For Marty."

"Gee. You and him must have been real good friends."

"I owed him some dough."

"You owed Marty?"

"Yeah. I talked to him this morning. He asked me to stop by and give the money to you. He also wanted me to tell you how sorry he was for some of the things

191

he did in the past."

"No kidding?"

"Yeah."

"You know, maybe Marty wasn't such a creep after all."

"Yeah."

I walked away from the waitress and headed toward the bathroom at the rear of the cafe. I stopped when I heard a familiar voice call my name.

It was Sherm Bolivia. "Toast!" he called from the front door.

A waitress behind the counter responded out of habit. "White or whole wheat?"

"Toast," Bolivia said in a lower voice when we met up near the bathroom door. "I've been looking all over town for you. Where've you been?"

"Where have I been? Where have you been, Sherm? You took a runner at Swale's church. I feel like you set me up."

Sherm took my arm and we went to the nearest table and sat down. He leaned across the table toward me. "Are you crazy, or what? I got bounced out of the place by a couple of goons. I figured they tossed you out, too and we just got separated. I waited at my car for an hour."

"You did, huh?"

"Yeah. Something different happen?"

"Much."

"Good copy for our story?"

"Stuff for my obituary."

"What are you talking about? Did they get rough with you?"

"Nothing I couldn't handle."

"Good, good. I figured you'd be okay." Sherm slapped me on the back and smiled.

"So, where have you been all this time, Sherm?"

"Me? Looking for you and working on the story. I've got a socko lead and about five hundred words. I'll show it to you when we leave here."

I looked at my watch. It had stopped. "What time is

it, Sherm?"

Sherm looked at his watch. "Going on seven."

"Shit! I'm supposed to be at Jan's for dinner."

"Jan? You mean Jan Thomas? I haven't seen her since...."

"I didn't know you knew her."

"I met her through you, Toast."

"You did?"

"Yeah, lots of times. Parties and things."

"Hmm. Jan never came to *COMET* parties. She wouldn't be caught dead at one."

"Well, then at a *Times* party. Or a Press Club bash, I don't know. I met her several times. Great gal. Damn good journalist, too. You shouldn't have let that one get away, Toast."

"My line broke."

"You got wheels?"

"No. I sort of got a ride here."

"I'll drive you out to Jan's."

"You will?"

"Sure, why not? Give you a chance to look over my lead."

I went into the bathroom to straighten up before we left the diner.

"My car's up that way," Sherm said, pointing over my shoulder, when we got to the street.

"Sherm. How did you know I was here?"

"I was driving by and I thought I saw you go into the restaurant."

"What luck, eh?"

"Yeah. Like I told you, I've been looking all over for you since we got separated."

"Bolivia the bloodhound. He always gets his man."

"You don't spend thirty years being a journalist unless you're part bloodhound. I thought you would have learned that by now, Toast."

"I've been learning a lot of things the last few days, Sherm. A lot of things."

"You're a sarcastic bastard, Toast. You know that?"

"Goes with the job, Sherm."

"Yeah? Well I don't care for it."

"Neither do I.

Once in the car I told Sherm how to get to Jan's. He reached into a briefcase and handed me the pages to his story.

Chapter 32

A weird religious cult believes Elvis Presley faked his own death and is in hiding waiting for the right sign to make a grand public reappearance.

The Jesus is in Galilee Church further believes that Elvis is the human form that the Second Coming of Jesus Christ will take.

Reverend Thurley Swale, the founder and leader of the Los Angeles-based cult told the COMET in an exclusive interview, "Elvis didn't die of an overdose of pills, nor was he killed by the CIA, or anyone else. He staged his own death. The signs that he did so and the sign that he is planning to return and begin his earthly ministry are plain for all to see if you know where to look."

There was more, but I stopped reading. I looked over at Sherm. "You interviewed Swale?"

"Well, it wasn't exactly an interview."

"Well, what exactly was it? You told me you got thrown out of the church."

"What's the big deal, Toast? It's good copy."

"I'm just curious about where the quote came from. Did you talk to him?"

"Look, Mr. Investigative Reporter, I didn't interview Swale. I pieced it together from his sermon and what you told me about him. Okay? Satisfied?"

"How could I not be satisfied with the *National*

195

COMET guidelines on accuracy?"

"That's right, college boy."

"But you know, Sherm, Swale didn't say anything about the CIA in his sermon and I didn't mention it in connection with him or the church. Where did it come from?"

"I'm in Westwood. Where do I turn?"

"Second right. Where did you get that bit about the CIA assassinating Elvis?"

"From you, Toast. You lost your mind or something?"

"I recall that you said it was a crazy notion and for me to drop it. What's it doing in the story?"

"It's good copy. You could learn from it. Tease the reader. Raise something tantalizing, dangle it for an instant and then—wham!—dismiss it. It's like a ten second blow job."

"Yeah, right."

I directed Sherm to Jan's apartment building. He pulled to the curb. I handed him his story and told him we should work on it in the morning.

"Hey," he said. "I don't want to spoil your evening or anything, but I'd really like to run up and say hello to Jan. You don't mind, do you, Toast?"

"Well, actually, Sherm, I do."

"Just to say hello. Take one minute. Less. Then I'm gone and you can get on with it. You'll have all night to get into her pants."

"When you put it that way, Sherm, how can I refuse?"

"Terrific!"

Sherm turned off the engine and we walked the half-block to Jan's building. The evening was warm and fragrant. The scent of night-blooming jasmine filled my nostrils. It smelled like nutmeg.

Jan buzzed us in. We took the elevator to the sixth floor and walked to her door and rang the buzzer.

The door opened. "Steve, darling," Jan said, reaching out to kiss me. "I'm so glad you...." She stopped when she saw Sherman Bolivia.

"Jan," I said. "You remember Sherm. From the *COMET*. He gave me a ride here. Wanted to pop in and say hello." I turned to Sherm. "Say hello, Sherm."

"Hi, Jan. Jeez, you look good."

Jan stepped back from the door. "Well, come in. The both of you."

She was carrying polite too far. "Sherm," I said. "Don't you you to be somewhere? Anywhere?"

"No," he said, barging past me into Jan's front room.

I looked at Jan and apologized with my eyes. Jan smiled and offered Sherm a drink. He took it.

"Just a little ice, Jan," he said. "Too much ice ruins a drink."

"How about you, Steve?" Jan asked. "What can I get for you?"

"Wine."

"White or red?"

"Both."

Jan laughed. She brought me a glass of chablis. She had one herself. She sat next to me on the couch. Sherm sat across from us.

"Nice place you've got, Jan," he said, making the smallest of small talk. I just buried my nose in my wine glass and blew small bubbles with my lips while I thought about other things and other places.

Five minutes later the doorbell rang. I looked up with a start. "Jan, are you expecting someone?"

She got up from the couch without saying anything and went to the door. She returned with a guy in a black windbreaker. He was wearing a pastel-colored shirt and an expensive pair of chinos. He looked like a cop or maybe an actor who plays cops in second-rate movies.

"Steve," Jan said. "This is Buckley Bergeron." I didn't stand up and I didn't shake his hand. I didn't know what was going on, but I didn't like it. I wanted to leave.

"Mr. Toast," Bergeron said, sitting down in a chair next to Sherm. "I will get right to the point."

I looked at Jan. "Right to what point?"

"You have something we want."

"We?" I looked at Jan again. She looked away nervously. I looked at Sherm. His eyes smirked back at me.

"A piece of clothing that once belonged to Elvis Presley. I think you know what I am talking about."

"Don't tell me you're a collector, too? Jan, what the hell is going on?"

"Sorry, darling. Better answer the man's questions."

I slapped my knee. "I knew it! I just knew it!"

"You knew?" said Jan, sounding surprised.

"I knew there was no job offer from the *Post*. And I knew you were being too nice for it to be true. It was a lousy act, Jan. A lousy, stinking act! I just didn't know the reason you were doing it."

"Well, now you do." She sounded as cold as bottled beer.

"Do I? What the hell. Why does everybody want Elvis Presley's goddamn jumpsuit? The last guy who tried to kill me said it was worth less than $100,000. True, that's more money than I'll ever see, but it's just crazy that people all over LA are killing each other for it."

Bergeron leaned forward in his chair. He lit a cigarette with a metal lighter. "Our reasons are different from the others," he said.

"Well, now we're getting somewhere," I said rolling my shoulders. "Would someone tell me where that is?"

Bergeron blew a puff of smoke toward me. The smell hit me first. It was strong, like a French cigarette. "We don't owe you an explanation. I am here to get the jumpsuit."

"For God's sake, Toast, tell him!" said Sherm Bolivia. It was more like a plea than a command.

"*Et tu*, Sherman," I said. "I knew you were pond scum as a journalist and I've always respected you for that. But this? What do you care about Elvis' jumpsuit? And who is this guy, anyway?" I motioned toward Bergeron with my head.

Sherm screwed up his face as if someone had

passed a bottle of ammonia under it. "Don't play stupid, Toast."

"I mean, what's in it for Sherman Bolivia? You wouldn't be here unless there were something in it for you. Am I right?"

"Toast, you're such a goddamn cynic."

"Don't be difficult, Steve," said Jan, sounding like she were reprimanding me for something as mundane as forgetting to take out the garbage.

I looked at her. "Jan. Good old ex-Jan. Just wanted me to make the right career move. Well, Jan, how am I doing?"

"We don't have much time," said Bergeron, impatiently. "Let's get on with it."

"No!" I said. "We have time. If you're anything like those other guys, you're going to dust me no matter what I do. I figure I don't have anything to lose, so we'll do things my way for a while. I want to know just what's going on here before I tell anybody anything. You dig? I looked at Bergeron, then Sherm, then Jan and finally back at Bergeron. "You can start by telling me who you are and why you want this stupid jumpsuit."

Bergeron looked bored by it all. "That is not possible. I work for the government and have been instructed to recover the garment. I can't tell you anything else."

"The government? What government? Our government?" Bells started going off in that tangle of wires and cables inside my head. "Where I come from, that could mean CIA."

"Just accept it, Steve," Jan said. "Just cooperate with Mr. Bergeron so we can all get on with our lives."

"Bergeron, Bergeron. I'm slow, but it's all starting to come into focus. I remember a story told me by a frightened little man on the run for his life. A story about a guy named Bergeron and two exile Cubans having dinner at Toots Shor's restaurant in 1977 and discussing a plan to assassinate President Carter. A story about how people who were at the restaurant that

199

night began dropping dead like bugs at a Black Flag trade show. It was a story that had a trail of bodies that led all the way to Elvis Presley. Was it a fairy tale or the truth? Who knows? The frightened little man said this guy Bergeron was CIA and the CIA was trying to kill him for what he knew. Are you that Bergeron? Did you kill that frightened little man?"

Bergeron reached inside his jacket. He pulled out what looked like a small electronic device. He said nothing as he began connecting a set of small wires to terminals on the device that was slightly larger than a paperback book.

I turned to Jan, who was wringing her hands. She looked uncomfortable. "And I also remember another story the frightened man told me. He told me about the time when the CIA's cover in the media was blown. When was it? 1977? I went to the *Times* library to check it out. That's one of the things I did there that night, Jan. Checking out the story of journalists acting as CIA informants and agents. The Washington *Post* was lousy with them. Seems it still is."

"There's nothing wrong with assisting your government," she spit at me. "There is absolutely no conflict of interest, either."

"Oh, you bet your cute wiggly caboose there isn't. You see the press as an arm of the government. In this case an arm of the CIA. Disinformation is the name of your game. It is worse than what we do at the tabloids. Much worse. I was coming here tonight to tell you, in a very nice way, to take your job offer and shove it." I tried to smile, but my face wouldn't cooperate.

A curved sneer crawled onto Jan's lips like a poisonous snake. "Don't lecture me on ethics, darling. You're nothing but a two-bit writer—I won't even use the word 'journalist'—working for a gutter rag. A comic book. What right do you have to tell me anything? What right? I work for the best newspaper in America. I make $85,000 a year. I have won two National Press Awards for investigative reporting. How dare you?"

"I rest my case." This time I managed a smile. I

turned to Sherm Bolivia. "Sherm. It is just the money, right? I mean there is no question of helping out Uncle Sam, is there? It's just the long green that interests you."

"Hey, Toast, I'm a journalist. I buy and sell information. That's what we do in this business in case you don't know. I write a story. I need some information. Without it, no story. I pay for the info if I have to. You bet your ass I pay. You do, too, Toast. You paid Coates for his story. The government or anyone else needs some information. If I've got it, I got it to sell. It's as simple as that."

"How long have you been on the take, Sherm? I'd really like to know."

"I've been working with various government agencies since the early '60s. You make it sound dirty. It isn't. And hey, they came to me, I didn't go to them. It's nothing personal against you, Toast. Nothing at all. You just got in the way."

"You paid piece-work, or what?"

"Just like we pay our sources. When this guy Coates showed up on the coast I was contacted that he might try to sell his story to one of the tabloids. They told me to keep an eye out for him. That's all I did. How much did you pay him, Toast? A grand? Two? See, it's the same thing. The exact same thing."

"No. There's a difference."

"No there's not."

"Buying and selling information is not the issue. It's who you buy it from and sell it to. When you are selling to the government, well, I guess it's like insider trading on Wall Street. It turns the whole business into a lie and a fraud. It makes what we do as journalists...."

Bergeron got up from his chair and stepped toward me. "That's enough. You can continue your seminar on ethical standards in journalism at another time."

"Will there be another time?" I asked.

"That depends on you. Produce the jumpsuit and you're free to bore anyone you like."

"I could be persuaded to cooperate if I could be

201

guaranteed I would walk away from this."

"I want the jumpsuit, Toast, not you."

"Sounds like a guarantee to me."

"Take it any way you like."

"Right. You might find this hard to believe, but I don't actually carry the jumpsuit around with me."

"Where is it?"

"It's in a storage locker at Union Station."

"Give me the key." Bergeron held out his hand.

"Uh, I don't have it."

"Don't jerk me around, Toast. People have ended up dead for being less of a pain in the butt than you are."

"There is no key. I mean a guy who works in the baggage room has it."

"And I suppose you're going to tell me that you have to be there in person so the man can identity you before giving up the key."

"You've heard this before?"

"We must watch the same television programs."

"The *Rockford Files*?"

"Whatever."

"Then we both know you are going to kill me as soon as you get what you want."

"Do we?"

"So where does that leave us?"

Bergeron looked at the device in his hand. "It leaves you just about to have a sudden and inexplicable heart attack."

"Ah, yes, the new CIA."

"Steve!" Jan shouted. "Please tell him!" She turned to Bergeron. "You didn't say anything about killing him. I won't stand for it."

Bergeron leered at her like he had just put his hand up her dress. "What are you going to do about it, lady? Write a penetrating expose for the *Post*?"

Jan got up from her chair and moved toward Bergeron. "Don't kill him! Please! He will tell you where the jumpsuit is." She rushed to me and grabbed my shoulders and began shaking me. "Toast, for once in your life don't be such a goddamn idiot. Tell him what he wants to know. What is it going to cost you?"

I knocked her hands away. "Didn't you hear the man, Jan? It doesn't matter. I'm dead meat, anyway you slice it. Look at it this way, babe. You'll be getting undisputed custody of the Trivial Pursuit game."

Jan tried to fight back the tears. "You're not going to give in are you?"

"Can't. I don't know where the jumpsuit is and old Buck here is too smart to fall for the old baggage-locker-at-the-train-station bit. No one believes me, but it is the truth."

Jan turned away from me and walked to Bergeron. "What if he really doesn't know? I believe him. He can't tell you what he doesn't know."

Bergeron pushed her aside. "Like the man said, it doesn't matter." Jan returned to a chair on the other side of the room.

She sat down and put her head in her hands. Bergeron looked at Sherm. "You, Bolivia, go down and bring your car around."

Sherm stiffened in his seat as if someone had dumped a pot of hot coffee in his lap. "Me? I don't want no part of this. I was just doing a job. I didn't sign up for this."

Bergeron was losing his patience. A thin line of sweat glistened on his upper lip. "Go get your car. Now! Or do you want to have a heart attack, too? It can be arranged quite easily."

Sherm slunk out of his chair and slithered out of the living room. I heard the front door open and close.

Bergeron walked toward me. "Put your hands out in front of you." When I did he clasped them in a pair of handcuffs that were held shut by some kind of velcro grip.

He went to the dinette and got a kitchen chair. He took it to the front window and sat down. He looked out periodically, looking for Sherm to bring the car around. I leaned back and waited, too.

This time I really did have it figured out. Armitage

was right about "S. B." And Coates was right about everything. About Bergeron, the CIA journalists, the plot to kill Carter and their murder of Elvis Presley. The CIA killed Coates for what he knew about them and to recover the jumpsuit. They killed Gilbert Talavera because he was on to them, or would have been in a matter of time. The CIA wanted the jumpsuit because it connected the Company to the plot against Carter and Elvis' death. How, I didn't know.

I didn't take any great satisfaction in arriving at the truth. It was a truth that strongly suggested that those paranoids who construct elaborate and convoluted conspiracy theories which insist that everything that happens in the world is connected and well-orchestrated, usually by evil nazis, the CIA, the Tri-lateral Commission, or murderous Soviet agents, are really the sane ones on the planet. It's the rest of us who are crazy for not believing them.

But what kind of world is it that can only be understood by paranoids who suspect every single thing that happens in life? What chance do the rest of us have if a small band of political extremists are running the world and nobody can do a thing about it because nobody believes they are the ones calling the shots? Something is wrong with this picture of the world. It is worse than the born-agains and their world-is coming-to-a-violent-end-at-Armageddon scenario. In both outlooks there is no hope for the species. What is going to happen is going to happen. It didn't matter if it was God or the nazis. It made my imminent heart attack a little more palatable, but only in a weird philosophical sense.

Chapter 33

I sat on the couch and waited with everyone else. My eyes shot hot steaming arrows of reproof at Jan. I didn't really mean it, though. I was beyond hating her. I did it to make her feel lousy. I mean someone had to do it for what she had done and I don't mean just setting me up. It gave me some pleasure that my evil stare got to her. She avoided eye contact with me and moved from place to place in the room like she was trying to get away from a bad smell.

Bergeron was growing impatient. I could tell by the way he smoked his cigarette. Me, I hoped Sherm Bolivia had been run over by a bus. I continued to annoy Jan.

"Say, Jan," I said, breaking a long silence. "While we're waiting for Sherm to come so old Buck here can take me out to some deserted arroyo and murder me, why don't we play a couple rounds of Trivial Pursuit?"

Jan stiffened and moved from her chair to a place near one of her book cases. "Stop it, Steve! I feel awful!"

"Come on, then. A game of Trivial Pursuit is just what the doctor ordered. Think of it as my last request. You, know, instead of a cigarette."

"You bastard! It's not my fault. If you weren't so goddamn stubborn."

"Believe me, I'd work on it if I had the time."

Jan wouldn't cry. She probably couldn't even if she

had wanted to. It didn't fit her career description. But she was close to it. She poured herself an eight ounce glass of white wine and began drinking it like it was fruit juice.

I was ready to start up on her when the door bell rang. Bergeron got up and stubbed out his cigarette in a glass ashtray that looked like a swan.

Bergeron was angry. "Why did he come back up here? He should have stayed downstairs with the car. Damn amateurs!"

He walked over to me and tapped me on the shoulder. "Time to go, sport. And please don't try anything heroic. I can kill you six ways from last Thursday before we reach the street."

I got up and walked to the front door with him. Jan buried her face in her wine glass.

Bergeron unlatched the door and turned the knob. The door exploded back into his face. The force knocked him into me and we both took backward half-gainers into the carpet. When I looked up I saw three men standing over us. Two of them were Reverend Swale and Twin Brother Osgood. They were pointing guns at us.

"Swale!" said Bergeron getting to his feet.

"Bergeron," said Swale, backing us into the living room with his gun.

"Twin Brother Osgood," I said, extending my tethered hands.

"Shut up!" he said.

"What happened to Sherm?" I asked.

Swale shook his head. "Mr. Bolivia turned out to be a great disappointment. I thought he was working with us. Imagine my surprise when he delivered you to the competition."

"You killed him?"

"No. He tripped over some trash cans behind the building. He has decided to spend the night there, but don't worry, Sherm Bolivia will live to sell out other colleagues." Swale looked around the room. "Let's all sit down, shall we?" He motioned to the chairs and the

206

couch. He looked at Jan.

"I'm sorry," I said, stepping toward Jan. "Reverend Thurley Swale, this is Jan Thomas. She set me up to be killed. Jan, Reverend Swale. He wants to kill me, too. You both have so much in common."

The muscles in Swale's face tightened into a frown. "You're getting to be something of a bore, Toast." He pointed to my handcuffs and nodded for Osgood to set me free. Osgood yanked open the velcro clasp.

"What are you doing here, Swale?" asked Bergeron. It was more an accusation than a question.

"Looking for the same thing you are, Bergeron."

"I've got the feeling that you guys know each other," I said, stating the obvious.

"We know each other very well," said Bergeron, looking at Swale.

"Since the Bay of Pigs," said Swale, looking at Bergeron.

"You guys are CIA, right? Then what's all the hub-bub?"

"Swale used to work for the Company," said Bergeron. "He's a renegade now. Been freelancing for years. How long has it been, Swale?"

"I lost track."

"The last I heard, you were running guns into Costa Rica for Ollie North."

"North dropped the ball on that one," said Swale. "Sunk our whole operation. I should have known better than to hook up with a Marine yahoo who really believes in God and country and all that rot. The ideological types. They're the worst. And North has an ego the size of Brazil. He deserved to take the fall."

Bergeron smirked. "It's just business with you, isn't it, Swale? Sell the guns to whoever has the price. Sell out your country to the highest bidder."

"Spare me the sermons, Buckley."

"Speaking of sermons," I interrupted. "What about Jesus is in Galilee?"

Swale smiled. "I was old school CIA, Toast. Ivy League and Catholic. I mean really Catholic. Ever hear

207

of Opus Dei?"

"Yeah," I said, unlocking a memory of the shadowy Vatican lay order that made headlines several years back as a conservative power force in the Holy See that was heavily involved with the Banco Ambrosiano scandal. It was a scandal that had rocked both the Vatican and the Italian government.

"I was a member for awhile. A lot of my family still is. This is not a sect of looneys. William Buckley and Bill Casey were among the initiated, just to name two. I was in it for both politics and religion. They go together so well, you know. Especially in the Catholic church. I took the religion very seriously in those days. I spent two years in the seminary before I started my career as a doctrinal subversive and got myself expelled.

"I really got into gnostic thought for a while. Jesus' faking of his death and Paul's merchandising of Jesus were a big part of that. It's great stuff and makes a lot of sense if you are interested in that sort of thing."

"I imagine you made a few bucks from the collection plate, too," I said.

"It provided a comfortable living, yes."

"My question is—why?"

"Why the Elvis thing? A lot of reasons, really."

"Don't you see?" said Bergeron. "It was his cover."

"Cover for what?"

"Right, Swale?" said Bergeron. "It kept you hot on the trail of the Elvis jumpsuit."

"I thought that was obvious."

Bergeron turned to me. "We've both been on the trail of the jumpsuit for the last two years. Swale has taken the creative approach. I prefer the more traditional way."

"And it led you both to me and Jan's apartment. How melodramatic."

"Take it any way you want," said Bergeron, dismissively.

I still wasn't satisfied. "I want to know why this jumpsuit is so important to the CIA and whoever you are working for, Swale."

208

Bergeron and Swale looked at each other. "You really don't know, do you?" asked Swale in a tone of voice that suggested I had just asked him what the letters "C. I. A." stood for.

"He doesn't need to know," snapped Bergeron. "You might find all this amusing, Swale, but I have a job to do."

"So do I," said Swale. "But you see, old man, I don't work for the Company anymore, so I don't care how much the man knows."

"Well, I bloody well do!" Bergeron's face showed the years of animosity that existed between Swale and himself.

"I am holding a .32 calibre gun and you are holding—what is it—one of your clever little devices that makes murder look like death by natural causes? Whatever it is, Buckley, old man, if it doesn't shoot bullets, then I'm afraid I have you at a disadvantage."

Swale turned to me. "You see, Toast, this whole thing started when your little friend ran away from home."

"You mean Coates?"

"Right. Only at the Company his name was Javert."

"Are you kidding? He told me someone from the CIA named Javert was stalking him."

Swale shrugged. "The Company drives people nuts if they stay around long enough. What can I say?"

"Coates took some classified documents with him when he left, didn't he?"

"Yes, indeed he did."

"You will pay for this, Swale," Bergeron threatened, cooly.

Swale smiled. "Actually, I believe you have that backwards, Buckley. Rather than paying, I will be paid. Paid for the jumpsuit. It is only a matter of time before I have it. I'm very close."

"What was in the files that Coates took?" I asked, remembering Gilbert Talavera's report about an operation called "Rainy Night."

"Very sensitive documents about acid rain, that's all," said Bergeron, jumping ahead of Swale.

"Shame, shame," Swale tsked. "For a file on acid rain, you wouldn't have gone to the expense of killing—how many people is it—I've lost count."

"We haven't killed anyone."

"Just like the Company didn't kill any of the witnesses to the JFK hit. They all died of natural causes, right?"

"Like Coates," I said. I still wasn't sure who killed him. The list of suspects still seemed to be growing.

"Yes," said Swale.

"No," said Bergeron.

"What?" I said, begging for clarification.

"Government agencies have been involved in acid rain research," said Bergeron, sticking to his story. "Like manufacturing it and experimenting with it in controlled situations. Not exactly chemical warfare, but in large enough quantities it can significantly disrupt a regional economy and alter human health patterns. Sensitive material, but not something the Company would kill for."

"Don't make me laugh," said Swale. "You and I both know the Company can and does kill people for not having the correct change if it suits their purpose".

"You're one cynical bastard, Swale."

"Me? Ha!"

I was beginning to get my fill of the personal stuff Bergeron and Swale had for each other. It sounded like The Odd Couple with licenses to kill.

I looked at Swale. "What do you say was in the 'Rainy Night' file?"

"You really don't know?"

"Will you quit saying that? Who am I? Philip Marlowe?"

"I may have overestimated you, Toast."

"A lot of people do."

"The file contained documents on the CIA and mafia collaboration on the Kennedy assassination."

"Forgive me, but that doesn't sound original. That

210

story has finally gone into the 'so what?' file, even at my rag."

"All the other stuff about the assassination is just clever speculation and Company disinformation. 'Rainy Night' is the smoking gun. It contains the real lowdown on Oswald, the identity of the tramps on the grassy knoll, the reason Kennedy's brain disappeared. Most important, it contains the chain of political buy-offs all the way to the Warren Commission. Who was silenced and how."

"Why would the CIA keep a file that was so obviously damaging to it? Why not destroy it?"

"The Company doesn't destroy anything. It hides things instead." Swale paused and looked at Bergeron. "Right, Buckley?" The CIA man just stared at Swale. He didn't say anything.

Swale continued. "If you know where things are hidden, you can turn up some very interesting things. It is a game with the Company. Like in the 60s and 70s when people were investigating each other looking for Soviet moles."

"And you knew where to look for things."

"I was one of them. It's one of the reasons I left the Company. I knew too much. It was only a question of time before I would have been arrested as a Soviet mole, tried, convicted and thrown into prison, where, no doubt, I would have been made to 'commit suicide'. I could see it coming."

"You're a raving paranoid," cracked Bergeron.

"Hey! You forget I worked in Counter-Intelligence under Angleton."

"James Angleton?" I interrupted. I wasn't totally ignorant of things.

Swale nodded. "James Jesus Angleton. The spook's spook. The man who was fooled by Philby and turned the Company upside down looking for Russian agents. He was the professor of political paranoia and I took his course."

Bergeron fingered his heart attack machine and quietly seethed while Swale continued to blaspheme his

211

employer.

"What does all this have to do with Elvis Presley's missing jumpsuit?" I asked.

"Your man took the 'Rainy Night' file when he left the Company. Or at least a microfilm copy of it. The man was a scared weasel. He had the file turned into microdots to make it easier to hide."

"How do you hide microfilm in a jumpsuit?"

"Microdots. Think about it. He had the dots placed under the rhinestones in the trim of the suit. Not a bad place to put them, I'd say."

"How did you find out where they were?"

"Was that when you killed him, Swale?" asked Bergeron.

Swale ignored the comment. "I went to his apartment just before you did, Toast. I saw you go in. I was in my car getting ready to leave. I found a notebook in his bedroom. It had a simple coded message in it. It was the kind of code the Company used in the 70s. It was changed a bit and it took me a while to figure it out, but I did." Swale turned to Bergeron. "How did you figure it out, Buckley? Poison it out of him?"

"I got it from your partner, the Bel Air collector. It was easy to get information out of him. He loves to talk about his passions."

"I should have covered my ass better. I thought he would be more help than he was. Next time—"

"I doubt there will be a next time."

I verbally stepped between Bergeron and Swale. "What are you planning to do with the microdots, Swale?"

Swale smiled and looked at Bergeron. "Oh, I don't know. If Bergeron is real nice I might sell them back to the Company."

"You're a real first class bastard, Swale. How did you ever last so long at the Company?"

The room fell into silence. People looked at each other and at nothing. Swale motioned to the big dummy standing next to Osgood. He walked over and Swale whispered something to him. He left Jan's apartment.

Probably went to bring the car around. I felt I was scheduled to take yet another ride.

Bergeron looked cool, calm and collected. A bit too calm, cool and collected for my taste. Jan blended in with the furniture and looked to be trying to think of ways to disappear altogether.

"What about the plot to kill Carter?" I said. "That's how Coates brought me into this thing in the first place." Swale and Bergeron glanced at each other.

"No such animal," said Bergeron, dismissively.

"The ravings of a dipso," Swale added.

"What the hell? What about Bergeron's meeting with the Cubans at Toots Shor's restaurant in January 1977."

"I don't remember any such evening," Bergeron said matter of factly. "I know a lot of Cuban patriots and I used to dine regularly at Shor's. If I was there in January of 1977, it was nothing more than an evening out with friends."

"What about all the deaths of the people who were there that night?"

"I haven't the faintest idea what you are talking about."

"Herbert Matthews, Freddie Prinze and Toots Shor himself."

"Matthews and Shor were old men."

"Oh, yeah? What about Prinze. He was 22."

"Suicide. Bullet to the head, I heard."

"Well, I know about the Rebounders."

Bergeron stopped. "Going to do me here?" Swale nodded." What about her?" Bergeron pointed to Jan. Swale sighed as if to say to her he was sorry, but she was in the way.

Jan didn't miss the meaning of his sigh. Her eyes doubled in size. For the first time she realized that her life, too, was in danger. It was one thing to feel sorry for a pathetic ex-lover who was on his way to oblivion, but when it came to her, well, it was more than her life that was at stake. It was her career. She began to hyperventilate. I thought she was going to have a heart attack.

"Toast!" she shrieked. "You bastard! You stinking bastard! I'm west coast bureau chief for the Washington *fucking Post*! I'm making $85,000 a year!"

Everyone stared at her for a long second before Swale pointed to Osgood. "Put her away," he said, calmly.

Osgood reached into his coat and pulled out his gun. From another pocket he produced a silencer and rapidly began screwing it onto the barrel of his gun.

Jan got her second wind. She began shrieking at the top of her lungs. She sounded like an Ethel Merman record being played backwards.

The fear in her eyes as Osgood raised his gun at her was nearly satanic. She was standing in the part of the living room nearest to the small hallway that led to the front door. She lunged at the light switch on the wall like a swimmer off a three-meter diving board.

The room snapped dark an instant before I heard the 'plop' sound of Osgood's gun. Someone said "shit!" I hit the floor and rolled until I was behind the couch. I heard the grunts of physical struggle, followed by several more plops from guns coming from different parts of the room. Then there was a thud near my feet. The front door opened. I heard running feet. Someone shouted "Swale!" It was Bergeron. Then I heard another pair of running feet. Then I heard nothing.

I heard nothing for a long time. It might have been five minutes. Then I took a chance and began crawling toward the front door. My way was blocked by someone lying on the floor. I recoiled like an opened oyster and continued along a different route toward the open door and the light in the outside hall.

When I reached the door I stood up. "Jan," I called into the dark room.

"Over here, Steve," she called back.

The lights came on. My eyes squinted. I saw Jan hugging the wall at the light switch. Brother Osgood was lying near the sofa with a big red mess on his head. Bergeron and Swale were gone.

"Steve, darling," Jan said when she realized both of

214

us were unhurt. She rushed me and threw her arms around my neck. "We're alive!"

"Yeah," I said. "This has got to be my lucky day."

Chapter 34

I didn't stay at Jan's very long after the shooting. Just long enough for a whisky to shake some of the fear from my bones. Jan wanted me to stay. She had saved my life and I was grateful. But she had also put it in danger. She had set me up like a row of bowling pins. She dangled a good job and good sex in front of me and then delivered me to a CIA hit man. I mean our relationship ended on a sour note and I have heard of the things partners do to each other to get revenge, but this was way out of line.

I told her that I didn't want either the sex or the job at the *Post* and furthermore, if she didn't return my Trivial Pursuit game I would see her in court. Then I left.

I actually felt good when I hit the street. I no longer had any strings tying me to a relationship that, with apologies to Yogi Berra, was over long before it was over. I was free from all that stuff they talk about on late night radio talk shows—guilt, anger, pain, responsibility. I felt nothing. Maybe that's what personal freedom is all about, I don't know.

I heard the police sirens as I walked up the street toward a bus stop. Someone must have called the cops when Jan was doing all that screaming. I smiled to myself picturing how she was going to explain a dead guy in her living room. But she was a serious journalist, she would come up with something.

I'm not sure how I could have explained Twin Brother Osgood's journey to the Promised Land. He could have caught a bullet intended for Bergeron. It was more likely that Bergeron managed to take the gun away from him and shot him with it. Then when Swale realized he was one-on-one with Bergeron, he must have decided he didn't like the odds and took a powder. Bergeron went out the door after him.

That was the easy part. It was just a matter of figuring out simple logistics. The hard part was the other stuff. The stuff that began the first time I met Coates.

I caught a bus going toward Santa Monica. It felt good to be on a bus going toward Santa Monica— Raymond Chandler's Bay City, the People's Republic Of, where Tom Hayden and Jane Fonda used to hang out.It is a boring landscape of yuppies and trendies. But it looked good to me as the bus chugged down Wilshire Boulevard toward the sea.

The bus was nearly empty. There were a couple of kids who were probably going to the Pier and a well-dressed matron who appeared to be both frightened and disgusted. She looked like the type who views public transportation as one small step away from homelessness and street crime.

I took a seat in the back and stared out at the closed shops and empty streets. This time I really and truly had it all figured out. It was simple. None of it ever happened to me. It was a five-day nightmare brought on by overwork or something I ate. That was the only way it all fit together. But I knew if it was a nightmare, it was the waking kind.

The problem was separating fact from fantasy; truth from speculation; reality from paranoia. That might not sound like too tall an order, but when you are a tabloid mucker living in that twilight zone they call Los Angeles and you are dealing in assassination conspiracies, faked deaths and Elvis Presley, believe me, it becomes a bit more difficult. Actually, it becomes a lot more difficult.

After five days of living nothing but this story, I

knew less than when I started. I didn't know who killed Coates, or why. Not really. I didn't know what secret information Elvis' jumpsuit held. I didn't know if there were CIA plots to kill Elvis or Jimmy Carter. And I didn't know if Elvis was alive or dead. Not bad for a week's work. Who said I didn't have the stuff to be an ace investigative journalist?

I got off the bus at Lincoln Highway. It was late and I didn't feel like waiting for the bus to Venice. I decided to spring for a cab. I started walking in search of a phone booth.

Was Coates a total paranoid who made the whole thing up? No, he did work for the CIA and too many of the things he told me checked out. Bergeron would lie to protect the CIA, but not Swale. I bought a lot of his story. But he said Coates was a nut case and there was no plot to kill either Carter or Elvis. No plot and no file about such a plot.

Swale said the file Coates took was the smoking gun to the Kennedy assassination. Was he telling the truth? Maybe he was covering his own role in the Carter-Elvis plot. Coates told me about Benny the Mixmaster, the master of disguise. He was the only figure I drew a blank on throughout this whole ordeal. Coates had drawn a blank on him. And so had Gilbert Talavera.

Was Swale Benny the Mixmaster? Could the bad blood between Bergeron and himself be traced back to a botched hit on Carter? Or was this another paranoid theory, too? My head ached with the possibilities. Nothing could be proven and almost nothing dismissed.

I saw a lighted blue phone kiosk up ahead. I walked over to it and opened the plastic cover of the phone book to look up a number for a cab. The pages listing taxi companies had been ripped out.

I began going through my pockets. I remembered having a card of a local cab company in one of my pockets that I kept for just such an emergency. I pulled out a small handful of papers from my pocket. One of the pieces was a small envelope. I looked at it. A telephone number not in my handwriting was on one side. I turned it over.

Coates! It was the envelope Coates had given me the last time we met. The number was his aunt's number. I had forgotten all about it. He said to call the number if anything happened to him. I looked at my watch. It was late. Coates had been dead three days. But I had to call the number. I dialed it slowly. I was sure I was getting someone out of bed. I was sorry, but this had to be done. I was convincing myself to hang up when a voice came over the line:

"This is Coates. By the time you hear my voice, Toast, I will be dead. Maybe now you will believe me. I haven't told you the entire story because you didn't pay for it. Where I am now I don't need money, so I can finish the story. Instead of telling you in this recorded message, I will tell you where you can find out the details for yourself.

"The entire CIA file known as Rainy Night has been put on microdots and placed under the rhinestone jewels of a performance jumpsuit once worn by the great Elvis Presley. Listen real good, Toast. I am about to tell you where I hid the jumpsuit. I want you to take the information contained on the microdots and write it up in your rag. We can blow the cover on the CIA once and for all. This is the biggest story of your life, Toast, so don't screw up. You can find the jumpsuit at ...."

There was more, but I hung up the phone. I was finished opening Chinese boxes and having my life threatened every time I got to a new box. I would have liked to have nailed the CIA and become famous like Seymour Hersh and Bob Woodward. I would like to have learned the truth about Elvis Presley's death. But the price was too high. I had been jerked around and bent out of shape by everyone I had come in contact with since meeting Coates. It happens to me a lot, getting jerked around and bent out of shape, but there comes a point when you've got to say "enough!". I had had enough of colleagues and ex-lovers using me for a pin cushion; enough of mind-boggling conspiracy theories that had turned me into a demented paranoid; and enough of guys I didn't know trying to kill me.

So, I was through with Coates and his story. Let someone else be famous. The Barfman would fire me, but that was a chance I was prepared to take. Something else I was prepared to take was a long vacation. Like a plane trip to the tropics. When I came back, if I could get my old job back at the *COMET*, I would request assignment on the "freak birth" beat or the "I saw Big Foot" beat. Or whatever. Anything but the Elvis watch. I would leave that to Sherm Boliva and the King's millions of fans. Elvis Presley would be around for a long time, whether or not he was still alive. Heroes die hard in America and Elvis would be alive and well in a cultural aspic until someone came along to take his place.

Maybe I would do something completely different. I might write screenplays for the movies. I hear there is money in that.

I fished around in my pockets and came up with the number for the cab company. I called and when the taxi came I told the driver to take me straight to LAX. My vacation had officially begun.

Gordon DeMarco is the author of the Riley Kovachs series of historical detective novels with political and labor themes. His first book, *October Heat* has been published in Britain, Germany and it is rumored, in Poland, where he has been promised many millions of zlotys.

He has written two popular history books on Los Angeles and Portland and has had three plays produced at the Edinburgh Festival Fringe in Scotland. He has also written a twice-weekly column on politics and popular culture for a small daily newspaper. He lives in a cabin near Portland, Oregon

Fiction

October Heat
The Canvas Priuson
Frisco Blues
Murder at the Fringe
The Five Pin Stands Alone (novella)

Plays

Who's Afraid of Abbie Hoffman?
Murder at the Fringe
Nocturne From Nowhere: Raymond Chandler On Stage

Non-Fiction

A Short History of Los Angeles
A Short History of Portland